PUSHING ON

A POST-APOCALYPTIC EMP SURVIVAL
THRILLER - THE EMP BOOK 3

RYAN WESTFIELD

Copyright © 2017 by Ryan Westfield

All rights reserved.

No part of this book may be reproduced in any form or by any electronic or mechanical means, including information storage and retrieval systems, without written permission from the author, except for the use of brief quotations in a book review.

Any resemblance to real persons living or dead is purely coincidental. All characters and events are products of the author's imagination.

1

CHAD

"We've got to get another vehicle," said Max. He was sitting up front in the passenger seat. He spoke his words with difficulty. His face was starting to swell up badly. "We're not going to be able to store enough gear in here. We're going to have to split up and take two vehicles."

"No shit," muttered Chad.

Chad, Mandy, Sadie, and James were crammed into the back of the Ford Bronco. It wasn't really big enough for them. Especially not with the gear left over from the Bronco's original owners.

Neither Georgia or Max had explained exactly what had happened. They'd just said that they'd gotten out alive. That was the important thing, said Max.

"Say something useful, Chad," said Mandy. "If you're going to say anything at all."

They'd left the granary and were headed into Albion, the tiny town in the northwest corner of Pennsylvania. So far, they hadn't seen anyone. No people and no vehicles. The town, so far, seemed empty.

But they hadn't yet gotten into the center of it.

"This is weird," said Georgia. She was driving. "I can't believe there's no one here."

"They could be inside their houses," said Mandy.

"There aren't any cars either," said Georgia. "It's like everyone's fled."

"Could be," said Max. "Let's keep our eyes peeled."

It was nerve racking, driving through the abandoned streets. There were houses all around them. They looked empty. But Chad knew that behind every window there could lurk someone with a gun. At every side street, Chad looked up and down both ways. His heart was pounding. He was just waiting for the attack that he knew would come.

"We shouldn't be driving into town," said Chad. "We've got to get back out into the rural areas. Isn't that what you're always saying, Max?"

"We need another vehicle," said Mandy.

Why was she always sticking up for Max and his ideas?

Chad's mind wasn't in a great place. He realized it, too. He realized he was getting bitter about Max making all the calls. Logically, he knew that Max tended to make the right decisions. It made sense that he was "in charge," if you could call it that. Still, Chad's mind was sinking into a dark place, and he couldn't shake the bitterness.

Chad knew he needed to calm down. He felt like his skin was crawling. His feet were freezing even though it wasn't cold out. The adrenaline was coursing through him.

They'd been through so much already. Who knew when the next attack would come. Who knew what terrible obstacle they'd have to face next.

And Chad knew he wasn't ready. He wasn't ready for any of it.

Chad was sitting with his hands around his bent knees, trying his best to look out the dirty Bronco windows.

James and Sadie were talking about something. Chad wasn't sure what. He wasn't paying attention.

Chad had lost the thread of the overall conversation between the other adults. They were probably taking about getting another vehicle.

The answer came to Chad by accident.

Georgia took a sharp turn. Something rolled out underneath Max's seat.

Chad knew right away what it was. He'd developed hawkish eyes for pills and drugs. After all, he'd spent most of his life high or trying to get high. By whatever means necessary.

It was a prescription pill bottle of Vicodin, Chad's favorite drug. It was the drug he'd been addicted to for years. He didn't even know how many. Max had given Chad's Vicodin to the dying man, and Chad had suffered horrible withdrawal. He'd enjoyed being clean. He really had. He'd been a different person.

But the stress was too much.

Chad palmed the rolling orange prescription bottle before anyone else even noticed it. His hands shook as he undid the safety cap. He shook a couple pills into his hand surreptitiously. He didn't bother to count them.

He had a moment of pause before he swallowed the pills. After all, the logical part of his mind told him not to do it. He couldn't go back to that place, that disgusting filth that was the addiction. He'd beaten it. He really had.

But while Chad had gone through withdrawal and

gotten clean, he'd never developed the coping skills needed to get through a stressful situation clean and sober.

And there couldn't have been anything more stressful that the collapse of modern society.

And the collapse wasn't over.

Hell, it might have just been beginning.

Chad swallowed the pill dry.

Almost instantly, Chad felt relief. Of course, he knew that the drug wouldn't actually get into his system for about another thirty minutes. It was mostly just placebo. Psychological relief, and nothing more. But Chad would take it.

His heart rate calmed down. His body became warmer. He felt ready to deal with whatever was coming. With pills, he could do anything.

Except when he could do nothing.

Chad knew the pills would come back to bite him in the ass. Probably in the worst possible moment. But that was later. And he just wanted to feel better now.

"There isn't a single car," said Georgia.

"Let's turn around, Mom," said Sadie.

"We've got to find another vehicle," said Max. "We have to keep going."

They were in the center of the town. Georgia had stopped at the main intersection.

Everything looked normal for a small town. There was a barbershop on one side of the street. A butcher. A small grocery store. Even a gas station.

But there wasn't anyone there.

And there weren't any cars. Not a single one.

"Let's drive through the rest," said Max. "We've gotta

find a car somewhere. Even if everyone fled in their cars, there's bound to be one left over."

"Yeah," said Mandy. "Aren't there like five cars for every American or something?"

"Something like that," said Georgia. "Do you really think we should keep going, Max? Maybe we should head out. I'm getting a weird feeling from this place."

"If we don't find a vehicle now," said Max. "I don't know where we're going to get one. This is perfect. Seems completely abandoned."

Georgia drove on through all the side streets off the main drag. The houses were small and tightly packed together.

This had never been a wealthy town. The houses had been for steelworkers, until the industry had changed. The economic devastation was palpable. The houses were in disrepair. The shutters were old and the windows cracked. The lawns were often neat and tidy, but the grass had died in patches, and there'd been no money to replace it or time to water it.

Chad was starting to feel *really* good. The Vicodin was kicking in. He felt warm and fuzzy inside. This was the feeling that he'd been craving for so long. He felt like he was on top of the world, like he could accomplish anything.

Of course, he knew that his reflexes would be slowed. His thought process would be muddled. If a crisis came, he knew that he couldn't rely on himself to make the right decision. Unfortunately, the drugs would trick him, and he'd *think* he knew what he was doing. A dangerous combination.

"There aren't any cars," said Georgia.

"Try the next street," said Max. "We've got to keep looking."

Chad's anxiety had left him. He felt happy for the first time in a long, long while.

Sure, it was a trick. It was just deception. But he didn't care.

"Look down there," said James, as they turned down a narrow street packed with houses. "There's something on one of the lawns."

As they got closer, they got a better look at it.

It was a car all right, but it wasn't even on the road. It was on someone's front lawn, up on cinder blocks.

"That's not going anywhere," said Max.

"Do you see that?" said Mandy.

"What?"

"That sign down there in that front yard. Another block down."

"A sign? We can't drive a sign," said Chad, giggling at the thought of trying to pack three or four people onto a sign and then take it down the highway as if it was a van.

"What the hell are you talking about, Chad?"

Chad didn't say anything. He was lost in his own little world, and he liked it.

"What do you see, Mandy?" said Max.

"It's like an advertisement for some car race or something," said Mandy.

Mandy had sharp eyes, and so did Georgia. Max probably couldn't see as well as before due to the swelling in his face, especially around his eyes.

"It's talking about a car convention or something," said Georgia.

"Yeah," said Mandy. "That's why I pointed it out. It

looks like whoever lives there is into those... what do you call them? Souped up cars?"

"Modded cars," said James.

"Yeah, those street racer types..."

"You think he might have a car there in that garage?"

"It's worth a shot," said Max. "If I had some kind of fast specialty car, I'd probably want to keep it safe if I had to flee my house for whatever reason."

"You don't think they'd take it with them?"

"Those types are crazy about their cars," said Mandy.

Georgia stopped the Ford Bronco in front of the house with the sign.

Chad look at the sign. It was neon green with a picture of a couple of modded Hondas on it. The sign seemed to swim in his vision, and he couldn't read the words very well.

The house was squat and somewhat broken down. If the occupant really had been a car enthusiast, and the sign wasn't some kind of mistake, then they'd put all their money into their cars, and none into fixing up the house.

"How do we know no one's inside?" said Mandy.

"We don't," said Max. "Come on. Georgia, Chad and I will go inside. The rest, stay in the car."

"You're not in any condition to go in," said Mandy.

"I'm fine," said Max, his words muffled from the swelling. His voice sounded strange too because of his broken nose.

Max and Georgia opened the heavy doors of the Bronco and got out.

"Chad," said Mandy. "Aren't you going with them?"

Georgia and Max were already approaching the house, their guns in their hands.

"Huh?" said Chad.

"What's wrong with you?" said Mandy. "You seem out of it. Come on, they need you."

She gave him a shove and it sparked him to open the door and get out.

Chad felt light as he walked towards the house, following Georgia and Chad.

Max turned back to Chad. "You're going to cover us from outside, OK?"

Chad nodded.

"Keep your gun up, damnit, Chad," said Max.

Chad suddenly remembered he was holding the shotgun that Georgia and Max had taken from the Ford Bronco's owners. They'd told him it'd be easier to shoot, and better for close range.

"Got it," said Chad. But he wasn't so sure.

He watched as Georgia and Max disappeared around the back of the house.

Chad found it hard to concentrate on keeping watch. The sun had come out from behind the cloud cover and with the temperature starting to cool off as fall approached, the day couldn't have been more beautiful.

There wasn't a person around to ruin the day by making some racket. There weren't any traffic jams or honking horns. There wasn't anything to worry about at all.

Chad caught himself. Nothing to worry about?

He had a lot to worry about.

He heard a sound around the back of the house. It sounded like a window breaking, like glass shattering.

He hoped Georgia and Max would be OK. He didn't exactly remember what they were doing, though. Something about breaking into the house to get something...

"Chad!" hissed Mandy, opening the Bronco door a

crack. "What the hell are you doing? You're supposed to be keeping watch."

"Oh," said Chad vaguely.

He'd sat down for some reason, on the warm, sunny green grass. He stood up and looked around.

Another sound came from around the back of the house. More glass shattering.

2

JOHN

"How long do you think it's been since the EMP?" said John.

"I don't know," said Cynthia. "I lost track so long ago. Sometime during the trip here."

"It was long," said John. "A few weeks, maybe?"

Cynthia shrugged. "No idea, really. It probably doesn't matter much."

"I guess not," said John. "It's not like we have to make sure we keep our dentist appointments or anything like that. But, still..."

He paused, looking for the words that didn't seem to come to him.

"What is it?" said Cynthia, prompting him to say more.

"It's just that... I guess I was still holding out a little bit of hope that the longer we got from the EMP, the greater the chance that someone would step in... You know? Like it was hard to believe that the whole country was affected, or the whole world. But if it wasn't, if things were running normally in other parts, then surely they'd step in and lend a helping hand."

"You mean like the military or the Red Cross would have dispatched or something?"

"Exactly."

"Well, we don't have any way to know what's going on anywhere else, without any communication. But I think the fact that no one else has come must mean that it's like this everywhere."

"I know I shouldn't have been holding onto even the smallest piece of hope," said John. "But I guess a part of me wanted it to be true."

"The thing we don't know," said Cynthia. "Is how other areas reacted to the EMP. It's possible that some places didn't become violently chaotic. Maybe they worked together to help each other."

"I doubt it," said John. "People are the same everywhere. And there's always that shadow of violence lurking beneath the surface. Modern society hasn't tamed us humans. It's just hidden what we really are."

"Do you think this one's any good?" said Cynthia, holding up a can of beef. It had a large bulge on the bottom.

They were in the basement of the farmhouse, going through the canned food that had been stored down there. Unfortunately, almost none of it was still good.

John shook his head. "Nope," he said.

"Save it for later, though?"

"Yeah," said John. "I mean, if things get really bad, I wouldn't mind eating that."

"It'll make you sick."

"Better than starving to death, I guess," said John.

But he wasn't so sure.

He'd had his fair share of sickness so far since the EMP, eating things that probably weren't good. But his stomach seemed to have gotten used to the bacteria somewhat.

The basement was dark, even during the day. They were using just one candle to illuminate the area, not wanting to waste their precious supplies.

They'd spent the last few days clearing out the dead bodies. There'd been at least a dozen of them, all shot dead. At first, they hadn't been able to figure out how they had *all* died from gunshot wounds. They'd thought maybe one of them had bled out from his wounds, after having killed the others. Then they'd realized that it was possible that there *was* a survivor, and that he or she had fled into the woods. And of course, that meant that this someone might return at some point, possibly to collect the gear left behind.

There was a lot of gear to sort through. There were more guns than they knew what to do with. There were backpacks and water bottles and protein bars and bags of food. Whoever these people had been, they'd been extremely prepared, not to mention armed to the teeth.

"Come on," said John, standing up. "I don't think any of this food is good. We've got plenty upstairs anyway."

"Good," said Cynthia, sighing. "This place gives me the creeps."

"It's just a basement. We've been through worse."

Cynthia shrugged. John could just barely see her gesture in the flickering candlelight. Since he'd met her, her appearance had changed. She'd lost some of the extra weight she'd been carrying. Her body had become lean and more muscular. She looked attractive, wearing a t-shirt that fit her tightly. They'd found it, along with other clothes, in the farmhouse.

At first, it had been difficult to figure out what had

happened at the farmhouse. John's brother, Max, had definitely been there, along with Chad. John still couldn't figure out what Chad was doing there. The only thing he could guess was that somehow Chad had wound up there accidentally. John couldn't see Max and Chad hanging out. They were too different. But Max probably felt some protective instincts towards Chad, even though he was, as they all were, completely fed up with him.

Once John and Cynthia had finished sorting through all the things in the house, they'd started to see patterns. Not everything could have belonged to the dozen men they'd found dead in the farmhouse. For instance, there were women's clothes, at least three sets. But there were no women's bodies to be found. The only logical thing to think was that Max lived there with other people, three of them women and one of them Chad. Who they were, John had no idea.

But it seemed as if Max and the others had left. Possibly they'd fled the dozen dead men. Or possibly they'd left earlier, and then the farmhouse had been overtaken by these gun-slinging mercenary types.

Many of the dead men seemed to have been convicts, judging by the crude tattoos that covered their bodies when John and Cynthia undressed them before dragging their corpses into the woods.

"We can't let anything go to waste," John had said. "We might need all this stuff."

"I know," said Cynthia, as they were trying to tug the pants off of a completely stiff corpse. "But this is just too... intense."

"We're going to have to get used to it," John had said. "There are going to be plenty more corpses."

"You don't need to tell me," Cynthia had said, making

John think of her husband's dead body lying in the yard. That had been when they'd met, and he knew that the memory wouldn't soon leave Cynthia.

John and Cynthia had taken everything they could find that was useful and put it in the large living room of the farmhouse. Finally, the farmhouse was starting to get organized. But it didn't look like it. At the very least it was free of dead bodies, so far as they knew. The gear they'd found formed huge piles in the living room. They'd done their best to sort through it, separating things into piles of weapons, food, clothing, backpacks, first aid.

They had so much gear that they didn't know what to do with it. Literally. Neither of them knew how to start a fire or shoot a gun. Cynthia knew a little bit about first aid, and John had enough common sense to know how to use a compass. But that was about it.

They'd been so hungry when they'd gotten to the farmhouse that they'd gorged themselves on the food they'd found. They'd eaten huge amounts of beef jerky. Their bodies had been craving animal protein. Finally, they'd had their fill of protein, and moved onto whatever sugary snacks they could find in the backpacks of the dead men.

"What do you think we should do?" said Cynthia, sitting down on the steps of the porch.

It was an all-too-common question. They must have asked each other the same question a dozen or so times each day.

And neither of them had an answer.

That was why they kept asking.

John, seated next to her, shrugged. He didn't even bother saying "I don't know."

There were too many questions that hung over their heads.

The sun was shining. The "yard" of the farmhouse, if you could call it that, looked beautiful.

They didn't know what month it was, but they knew fall was approaching. A couple of the trees had started to change their shade of green. The air had a bite to it at night, and the slightest chill crept into it during the day.

They remained silent for a long while.

Finally, John spoke. "I think we should see if there's anybody else in the area."

"Are you crazy? You mean more people like the ones we found in the house? Mercenary types? People with guns?"

John shook his head. "No," he said. "I mean friendly people. People who can help us. And maybe we can help them. We're going to need to team up with others if we're going to defend the farmhouse."

"So you think we should stay there, then?"

"What choice do we have? We have nowhere else to go and no way to get there."

"Maybe we could find a car. You know, find a car and some gas."

John shrugged. "Maybe," he said. "That'll be our backup plan. This place just seems too perfect in a lot of ways. And we've got all this gear. All these guns."

"We need to figure out how to use those, by the way."

"I know," said John, nodding. "Have you ever shot a gun before?"

Cynthia shook her head. "Have you?"

"Nope. I mean, I've never had a problem with them or anything. I just never got around to it, I guess. I probably should have, though."

"Same for me," said Cynthia. "My brother used to go shooting with my dad as a kid. They invited me along, but I never wanted to go. It didn't exactly fit in with my interests at the time."

"Let's start now," said John. "We can learn. How hard could it be?"

"Right now?"

"We've waited too long, anyway," said John. "And if we're going to go exploring the area around here, we'd better be armed and we'd better know how to use the guns."

Cynthia nodded. "OK," she said.

They had an enormous stockpile of weapons left over from the dead men. There were a couple hunting rifles, some assault rifles, a shotgun, and about a dozen handguns, of all different types.

As far as identifying the guns, John and Cynthia were at a loss. They knew the basic types and not much else.

"I think this one is a revolver," said Cynthia, picking up one of the pistols.

"Careful with that," said John. "Make sure to keep it pointed away from anything you don't want to shoot."

"Sorry."

"It's OK. But we've got to be careful. We can't deal with a gunshot wound."

"Yeah, that's the last thing we need."

John regarded the gun Cynthia was holding. "I don't think that's a revolver," he said. "Look, it loads from the bottom, not the side, like in those cowboy movies."

"I want a revolver," said Cynthia.

"What's the difference?"

"I don't know. It seems more 'classic' I guess."

John laughed. It was the first time he'd laughed in a long time. "Still thinking about being stylish."

Cynthia smiled at him. "Come on, let's go shoot some cans in the yard or something."

They took the guns and the ammo out into the field and spent some considerable time becoming familiar with them. They had to work off their instincts, common sense, and what they'd seen in the movies. They started off slow, just getting familiar with the handguns. They decided they'd leave what seemed like the more complicated guns for later.

"This isn't that hard," said Cynthia, as she pointed her revolver at an old empty can of beans they'd set up on a rock.

"Don't get cocky yet," said John. "You still haven't shot anything."

Cynthia winked at him before turning back to the can. She stood with her legs apart and the gun in front of her. She was smart enough not to try anything fancy or unrealistic, like the heroes in action movies sometimes did, holding the gun sideways.

She squeezed the trigger.

Nothing happened.

"Safety," said John.

Cynthia cursed. She flipped the safety, and she was ready.

She aimed the gun, and pulled the trigger.

She missed.

John's ears rang. The shot was much louder than he'd expected.

"Shit," said Cynthia, speaking very loudly. Even so, he could barely hear her. "This thing kicks like crazy."

"I didn't realize it'd be so loud," said John.

"What's that?" shouted Cynthia.

"Loud," shouted John.

They'd need something to protect their ears if they were going to practice more.

John had a vague idea that some guns were louder than others, but he didn't know which ones were which.

Later, the ringing in his ears had died down enough to not have to shout.

"I'm going to head out today," said John. "Start off small. Just explore what's immediately around here."

"Don't think you're going alone," said Cynthia.

"It might be dangerous."

Cynthia shrugged. "It's dangerous staying here alone. So far, we've just gotten by on the good luck that no one else has showed up. If someone comes when you're gone, well..."

"Not sure how much help I'd be if I were here," said John.

He didn't feel confident in his abilities to defend himself. But he knew that he'd try. He'd done it before, using only a knife. So long as he learned a little more about how to use a firearm, he'd be even better prepared than before.

At least he had the willpower. And the desire. He'd already proven that.

"Fine," said John. "You're coming with me then. We'll take a small backpack each, with food and water. Extra ammo. The first aid kit."

"Why bother with all that stuff?" said Cynthia.

"Who knows," said John. "We might find ourselves in a situation where we can't get back to the farmhouse."

"Let's hope not," said Cynthia. "It's already starting to feel like home."

John knew what she meant, but he didn't think about it quite like that. If anything, the house should have had more sentimental value to him than Cynthia. After all, it was his family's, and he'd been there as a kid. But John had never been a sentimental person. Maybe it ran in his family. They were practical people, usually. It was just that John's practicality had, for most of his adult life, run him in the direction of earning a lot of money. And that money wasn't going to do him any good now. It was gone, nothing more than the memory of numbers on a computer screen.

To John, the farmhouse meant a practical structure, away from the city and the suburbs. It was a place where they might be able to forge new lives. But he knew they'd need some help. More people were bound to show up, and John and Cynthia didn't even know how to shoot yet.

"What are we going to do if we come across someone?" said Cynthia. "Someone who wants to hurt us?"

"Point and pull the trigger," said John. "And hope for the best."

3

MAX

Max used the butt of his pocketknife to shatter a glass window of the basement. It was one of those houses built on a hill, so that the basement was above ground and exposed on the rear end of the house.

"What's the plan?" said Georgia. "What if someone's inside?"

"It's a risk," said Max. He left it at that.

Max used his elbow to knock out the glass that remained in the pane. He shined his flashlight—which he tried to rarely use because of the battery—into the dark basement.

"I don't see anyone," he said. "But that doesn't mean much. They'd have heard the glass shattering, obviously. I'll go first."

Georgia seemed to know better than to argue with Max.

Max was badly bruised from the fight. Everything hurt. The best way for him to keep his mind off the pain was to keep active. Both his body and his mind. That'd always been the way he was. He'd felt so frustrated at his job, before the EMP, partly because all the work was directionless. Pointless. Now he had a purpose. A real one.

Gun in hand, Max squeezed his way through the narrow window.

"Looks clear," said Max.

He kept his eyes glued to the staircase as Georgia worked her way through the window.

"Musty," she said, curling up her nose and sneezing. "It has that feel of a house that no one's lived in."

"Well, we can't go by that," said Max.

Georgia gave a stiff nod.

The basement was sparsely furnished. A set of free weights and a bench sat in one corner, looking like it'd been collecting dust for a long time. A door led to the garage, which was built into the basement.

Max motioned for Georgia to cover him, threw open the door, and moved into the garage swiftly, leading with his Glock.

His flashlight illuminated the pitch-black garage. There was a car. That was good. But before celebrating, Max checked the other side of the car, as well as underneath it.

It was clear.

"Good news," said Max. "But stay out there, in case someone comes down the stairs."

Max knew that the house was most likely completely abandoned. But there wasn't any sense in taking chances when they didn't have to.

"Does it run?"

"I'll check."

This was a car that had spent the majority of its life in the garage. There didn't seem to be a scratch on it. It wasn't exactly Max's style, not that that was important in the least.

It was a Honda Civic, souped up. The muffler was huge, and when Max, finding the keys on a hook, cranked the engine, the sound was almost deafening. The owner had likely removed the catalytic converter for better airflow. The sound of unfiltered exhaust began to fill the garage.

Max checked the gas gauge before quickly killing the engine. After all, the garage door was still closed.

There was gas.

"Looks like we have our second car," Max said.

"Should we check the rest of the house for provisions?" said Georgia.

Max agreed, and together they moved swiftly through the rest of the house, clearing each room. It wasn't a large house, and it didn't take long.

Only after assuring themselves that there was no one hiding under a bed or in a closet somewhere, waiting to attack them, did they start looking through the house for things that could be useful to them.

"Aside from the car," said Georgia. "This is a bust."

"Yeah," said Max, looking through the kitchen cupboards. "Looks like whoever lived here took just about everything useful you could think of."

"Let's head out. Think they'll be excited to see the new ride?"

"James will. He loves those types of cars."

Max laughed, and it made his face hurt. The huge guy he'd fought had hurt him bad. But Max had hurt him worse. And that was what was important.

Whoever was still alive was the winner.

Back in the garage, Max threw open the door. Light poured in, shocking their darkness-adjusted eyes.

Max put the Honda into reverse. It had a short, stubby aftermarket shifter, as well as all sorts of extra dials on the dashboard.

"You think this thing'll be reliable?" said Georgia. "Sometimes these are great for going fast, and not so good at not breaking down."

Max shrugged. "It's all we've got. Unless we find another car."

The Honda moved faster than Max had expected. Even in reverse, just tapping the accelerator lightly sent the car zooming out of the garage. Max had to slam on the brakes just to keep from going too far off the driveway.

Max brought the car up to the Ford Bronco, where everyone was waiting.

"Holy shit," said James, getting out of the Bronco. "Nice ride."

Mandy laughed nervously when she saw it.

"I just hope it works," said Georgia.

Something seemed off to Max. Something was wrong.

It hit him suddenly. "Where's Chad?"

Chad was nowhere to be seen.

Everyone spun their heads around.

"Shit," muttered Mandy. "That asshole's left us."

"No one was watching him?" said Max.

"I was watching the street," said Mandy.

"Me too," said James and Sadie together, looking guilty.

Max couldn't chastise them. You couldn't expect people to watch the guy who was watch.

"Chad's been so much better since stopping the pills," said Max. "This doesn't make sense."

"Maybe someone took him," said Sadie.

"Like kidnapped him?" scoffed James. "Why would they do that? Plus, we would have heard something."

"We've got to find him," said Max.

"Let's just get out of here," said Mandy.

"We can't leave him," said Georgia.

"Remember, Mandy," said Max. "He saved our lives back at the farmhouse. We're all going or no one's going."

"So what do we do?"

Max didn't say anything.

The truth was that he didn't have the slightest idea, short of going around the neighborhood looking for Chad like he was a lost dog.

4

JOHN

John and Cynthia had been walking alongside the rural road for the last twenty minutes. They kept mostly within the tree line, in case a car passed by.

So far, they hadn't seen anyone. John hoped it would stay that way.

"I wish I knew how to use this thing," said Cynthia, holding up her handgun.

"Put that down," said John. "You're going to shoot one of us by mistake."

"I've got the safety on... I think."

"Wow," muttered John. "Here, look, don't put your finger inside this guard around the trigger. Not unless you're going to shoot someone."

"Makes sense," said Cynthia, nodding, returning the gun to its holster. "How'd you figure that out?"

"Must have picked it up somewhere. Wait."

He grabbed her arm and held her.

"There's someone up there," whispered John. "In the woods. Do you see them? Stay still."

Up ahead, there was the faintest bit of movement. A flash of a color. Synthetic, definitely not natural.

"Yeah," whispered Cynthia. "I see them. What do we do? Run?"

"I don't know."

"Let's wait," said Cynthia. "See who they are."

They ducked down, out of the way, behind a large tree.

Five minutes later, they could see them. A man and a woman, each with a large hiking backpack.

"They don't look dangerous," whispered Cynthia.

"I don't know..."

John's gut was telling him not to be afraid. The pair was in their mid-twenties. If it hadn't been for the EMP, they would have looked like normal hikers, not out of place on any serious trail in Pennsylvania.

But John's brain was telling him that he needed to play it safe.

The hiker couple didn't look like they were armed. They didn't look like the types—not that that meant much these days.

John and Cynthia stayed hidden.

"What do we do?" whispered Cynthia.

John didn't answer. He didn't want to give away their position.

Instead, when the sound from the hikers got louder, John rose into view, pointing his handgun at them, holding it as steadily as he could.

"Don't move," he said loudly.

Cynthia rose up and copied John, holding her gun out too.

"We don't want any trouble," said the man.

"Hands in the air," said John.

They did as he said.

John got a better look at them now that they were close. The man had close-cropped hair. The woman was pretty, with long blonde hair tied into a ponytail. They both wore wedding rings.

John had changed. Weeks ago, he'd been living the high life in Center City. He'd been the one someone would have tried to mug. Now he was pointing a gun at strangers.

But he'd been through a lot.

Cynthia glanced over at John expectedly. She was waiting for him to do something.

John had to figure out how to determine if they were a threat or not.

They certainly didn't look it.

But how could he tell just by talking to them? Just do the best he could, he guessed.

"What are you doing out here?" said John.

"Same as you, I guess," said the man. "I'm Derek, and this is Sara. We're from the suburbs. We decided to hike out when things got bad."

John nodded.

"You armed?"

"I wish I was," said Derek. "But unfortunately no."

"Put your packs down," said John.

John moved over, keeping the gun trained on Derek, and grabbed the packs. He kicked them off to the side. They were heavy, loaded down with gear, and likely food. Gallon water bottles dangled off the sides.

John wasn't going to let his guard down, even though the vibe he was getting from these people screamed "normal people, not a threat."

"Keep your gun on them," said John to Cynthia.

Keeping his own gun on them, he patted them down

one by one, checking everywhere he thought a gun might be hidden. Waistband, under the arm, the ankles.

"Looks like they're clean," said John.

Since there might be a weapon in the packs, and knowing that it would take a long time to go through them, John pushed the packs farther away.

"You can relax," said John. "Let's sit down and have a talk."

"Awesome," said Sara. "I'm beat. We've been walking forever." She threw herself down on the ground, and Derek did the same.

"Sorry about all that," said John. But he kept his gun in his hand.

"No worries," said Derek. "We know how it is. Everyone's gone crazy. You don't know who to trust."

John nodded. "Tell me your story. Where are you coming from?"

"Ardmore," said Sara. "And we're headed out as far as we can get. We've been hikers forever, so this seemed like the natural route. We already had all the gear."

"We hike the Long Trail in Vermont every year," said Derek. "That's actually how we met."

They seemed like nice, honest people. The more they talked, the more John found himself trusting them. And they really didn't seem to mind the guns. Maybe Derek and Sara had a good read on people, and could sense that John and Cynthia weren't going to murder them for their possessions.

Derek and Sara told them what it'd been like in the suburbs. They'd stayed through the formation of the rogue militia, the same group that had tried to kill John. The group that had murdered Cynthia's husband.

"I went through there myself," said John. "It seemed

like it was made up of military guys? The police? It just didn't make sense. I mean, I knew guys in the service, and cops too. They were good men. And women."

John shook his head. "I mean, it was a mix. There were some military guys, some cops. There are bad eggs in any basket, you know? A lot of the guys that we saw in the militia were actually criminals. They'd escaped from the penitentiary. Others were just scrounger types, nobodies who'd been waiting for a chance to break through and have things their way. And the guys who'd been cops, a lot of them just figured they were doing the right thing. Trying to keep things under control and all that."

"They did some horrible, horrible things," said Sara, her face contorting in the memory of it all.

John looked at Cynthia briefly, but she didn't seem to want to relive the memory of her husband's death by talking about it. Not now, at least.

"The real problem is the leader," said John. "Apparently he was in the joint for years and years. You've never seen someone like him. Missing half his teeth. Tattoos all over him. Just huge. Spent all his years locked up working out. He'd gone in for a triple homicide. Goes by the name Kor. Don't ask me what it means. Some kind of prison nickname, I don't know."

"You saw him?" said Cynthia, sounding scared.

"Well, not personally. Or we probably wouldn't be here. But the rumors were crazy."

"Do you know anything else about him?" said John.

John knew that the more information they had, the better off they'd be. Even though the rogue militia was far away from them, they could still be a threat.

"Well," said Derek. "The word is that they're looking for communication devices."

"Communication devices?" said Cynthia. "You mean like cell phones? I thought everyone knew those don't work."

Derek nodded. "They don't."

"The towers aren't going to work," said John.

Everyone nodded.

"Right," said Derek. "But a shortwave radio would work."

"It'd have been ruined in the EMP," said John. "It was so powerful that even small electronic devices were affected."

Derek nodded. "They're looking for one that was shielded by a Faraday cage. You know, a metal cage inside another metal cage. It blocks all electromagnetic signals."

"Who would have put their shortwave radios in a Faraday cage?" said Cynthia.

"Well, people who were very prepared," said Derek. "But think about it, not that many people have shortwave radios to begin with these days. They're pretty rare."

"So what's the deal? What does this Kor guy want with a shortwave radio?"

"Rumor is he thinks he can gain more power," said Sara. "Basically he wants to expand his little empire. And unfortunately, he's pretty savvy. He knows that communication is going to be crucial for what he wants to do."

"Shit," muttered John. "This isn't good."

"At least we're pretty far away," said Cynthia.

"I don't know how much good that's going to do," said Sara. "Word is they're sending scouting parties out. We narrowly avoided one of them."

"You're lucky to be alive," said John. "Hiking all the way out from the suburbs. We did the same thing, but it was tough."

"We know all the little trails," said John, giving a half-smile. "Better than most."

"Sounds like you're pretty prepared yourselves," said John. "I had nothing when I started out."

"Well, in a way, yeah. But we need weapons."

John thought for a moment. They seemed like good people. And they were pretty relaxed and easygoing, considering the situation. He knew they weren't going to try to hurt him or Cynthia.

"Maybe we can help you out with that," said John. "But what are your plans? Staying around here?"

"No," said Derek, shaking his head. "We're going to keep going."

"We want to get out as far as we can," said Sara.

John frowned. He wondered if he and Cynthia should be doing the same thing. Maybe the farmhouse wasn't the best option.

"You can help us get weapons?" said Sara. There was eagerness in her voice.

Looking at her, no one would have ever thought she'd be so enthusiastic about the possibility of getting a firearm. Even with the dirt from weeks on the trail with no bathing facilities, she still had a glimmer to her. Derek did too. They looked like they'd been living quite the life back in the suburbs.

"We have a lot of guns," said John. He explained how they'd arrived at the farmhouse to find all those dead bodies, and he told them about the guns. "I don't see the harm in parting with two of them. There's more than we can use. But would you consider staying at the farmhouse with us? There's room to grow food. And we could use more people to help us defend it."

"That's tempting," said Derek. "The thought of continuing on, and not knowing what's coming next is tough."

"Very tough," said Sara.

"Why don't you come over, rest for a little while? Get a good night's sleep in a real bed, and then decide in the morning. No pressure."

"Deal," said Derek and Sara together.

They all shook hands and grinned as best they could at each other, considering the grim circumstances.

"Hey," said Sara. "Do you hear that?" She perked her head up, almost like an animal.

They all fell quiet.

"Sounds like a car engine," said Cynthia, speaking in a low voice. "A big one."

John motioned for everyone to move farther away from the road.

Could it be that the militia had sent a scouting party out this way already?

Really, it could be anyone. With any intentions.

To John's horror, the car didn't keep going. From the sound of the engine, the vehicle had clearly stopped. Right near them.

"What do we do?" whispered Derek.

John held up a hand, letting them all know to stay quiet. His knuckles were white from gripping his handgun. He wished he'd spent more time practicing before venturing out from the farmhouse.

There was the sound of a door opening, and slamming closed.

Shit.

5

MANDY

"We've got to find him," said Max. "We'll split up. Mandy, you come with me in the new car. Georgia, you take your kids in the Bronco. We'll meet back here in twenty minutes. Keep your eyes peeled. And your hands on your guns."

"What if we don't find him?" said Sadie. She seemed worried about Chad's fate.

Mandy wasn't worried about him.

She felt guilty about it. But as far as she was concerned, losing Chad would actually be a benefit to the whole group.

Sure, he'd saved their lives one time, as Max had said. But how many other times had he put their lives in danger? And how many more times in the future?

"We'll find him," said Max. "But if we don't, we'll move on."

Mandy was surprised. So far, Max had done everything he could for Chad. Hard love, though, that was what he'd given him.

Then again, Max seemed like he'd do almost anything for any of them.

Mandy looked at Max's battered face, badly bruised, and wondered just how far he'd be willing to go for them. And for her.

"Come on," said Max gruffly, as he got into their new vehicle.

This wasn't the time for pretty words. This was the time for action.

The car was lower to the ground than a normal car. It took Mandy some effort to get into the passenger's seat.

"This is our new car?" she said, examining the flashy interior. Not just the dash was altered. The seats were aftermarket, too, those racing bucket style seats, with seatbelts meant for track-only use. On the rear windshield there were all sorts of logos and stickers.

"It's what we've got," said Max, cranking the engine. "It's too low for going off-road, unfortunately. And it'll probably be terrible on gas. But the acceleration might come in handy. Maybe."

"Hopefully not," said Mandy. "I don't know what we'll do if we run into guys like those scary guys in the Ford Bronco."

"What do you mean?" said Max. "We'll just do have we have to do. No sense in worrying about it now."

"You're always so pragmatic. So practical."

"Worked so far," was all Max said.

Mandy glanced in the side mirror, watching as Georgia drove the Ford Bronco slowly in the other direction.

The Honda was almost unbearably loud as they drove down the block.

"Look everywhere," said Max. "Who knows where he'll be."

"Why would he just wander off?" said Mandy.

Max didn't answer.

The sun had gone behind the clouds, and the neighborhood was looking practically dismal under the gray sky. The people who'd lived here had been hard workers. They'd done long shifts, when there was work to be found. They hadn't had the time or money to spruce up their yards with fancy gardens or shrubbery. The houses were unadorned. Practical and neat, but not fancy.

Max drove down the street and took a turn. There were a couple more trees on this block, but mostly it was more of the same.

Just when Mandy was thinking they'd never find Chad, there he was.

Chad was standing in the middle of a front yard, staring up at the sky. He clutched something in his hand.

Max parked the car and got out.

"What the hell are you doing?" shouted Max.

"Huh?" said Chad.

He spoke in a weird way. He didn't slur his words, but his voice sounded different.

"I thought we'd finally lost you," said Mandy. "Why the hell would you wander off? You put our lives at risk."

Max raised his hand, signaling to her that enough was enough.

"Are you OK, Chad?" said Max, examining Chad for signs of injuries. He stared into his eyes.

"Your pupils are contracted."

Chad just nodded.

"He's using again," said Mandy. "Opiates make the pupils contract."

Mandy was disgusted. How could Chad revert to his old self? Sure, she hadn't liked him either way. But he'd been doing a lot better.

"Impossible," said Max. "Where would he get anything?"

"Who knows," said Mandy. "Addicts are resourceful when they want to be. When they need their fix."

"I don't think it's likely," said Max. "Maybe he's cracking under the stress."

"I'm fine," said Chad. He finally looked at them, but the dazed look didn't leave his face.

"What has he got there?" said Mandy.

She impatiently grabbed the paper that Chad held in his hand. She had to really tug on it to get it out.

"It's just some kid's school report," said Mandy, glancing at it. "Fat lot of good this'll do us."

Max took it from her and began reading it.

"Don't waste your time with it," said Mandy.

"Look," said Max, pointing at a line. "It's a school report, all right. But it might be useful. See here? It says that this kid's grandfather lived on a farm in Kentucky."

"So what?" said Mandy.

"The farm's been in the family for years," said Max, continuing to read the simplistic school report. "There's no one living there, and it's not near anything. It's way out in the middle of nowhere, some rural part of Kentucky. I think this might be our next plan. We'll head a little bit south."

"Are you serious?" said Mandy.

"Sure," said Max. "It's all here."

"But it's just some report. Maybe he made it all up."

"Let's check the house. Maybe there's more information. Chad, where'd you get this?"

"Living room," mumbled Chad.

Max checked his watch. "We still have twelve minutes before reuniting with Georgia. Come on, let's move."

Mandy followed Max towards the house.

"You coming, Chad?" said Mandy.

He just nodded vaguely and stayed where he was standing, swaying a little.

"I don't know where you got whatever it is," said Mandy. "But you're definitely on something. You're not fooling me."

Chad didn't respond.

Mandy's grip instinctually tightened on her rifle.

"You think Chad broke a window?" said Mandy. "How'd he get in?"

The house looked almost identical to the one they'd gotten the Honda from. The only difference was that it was missing some shutters on the windows. Whoever had owned it probably hadn't had the money to replace the ones that had fall off.

"Looks like he just went through the front door," said Max, as he turned the knob and the door opened. "They probably left in a hurry. Didn't even lock up."

The house was a mess. Clearly the former occupants had scrambled to get ready, leaving their possessions strewn around.

In the living room, as Chad had said, the rest of the report sat on a coffee table in front of the couch.

"It's still just a report," said Mandy, picking up the papers. Most of what she saw were just first draft versions. Chad had taken the final draft, the one without as many spelling errors.

"But look at this," said Max. "It's real. There's the deed to the land and everything."

He showed it to Mandy. It looked real all right.

"Damn Chad," muttered Mandy.

"You think the others will go along with it?" said Max.

"Why are you asking me? They'll do anything you say."

Max didn't say anything.

They briefly looked through the rest of the house. There wasn't much that they could use. The kitchen had been emptied. The food in the fridge and freezer was rotten.

They left, somehow got Chad into the back seat, and drove back to the house they'd gotten the Honda from. The neon sign out front made it easy to recognize.

The Ford Bronco was already there, waiting for them.

"You found him," said Georgia, getting out of the Bronco. She sounded relieved.

"Yeah," said Max. "But he seems shocked. I don't know what happened to him."

"He's messed up on drugs again," said Mandy.

Georgia frowned.

"Either way," said Max. "We've got to keep a close eye on him."

Mandy wondered if Georgia was on her side in thinking that Chad was becoming more of a liability by the minute. Even Georgia's kids were way more competent at just about everything, except when it came to brute strength. Chad was good for moving heavy things.

Mandy knew in her heart she wasn't a cruel person. She wouldn't have been able to leave Chad behind, if she'd been given the choice.

But wasn't it normal that she felt some resentment towards him?

It was their lives that were at stake, after all.

"So we've got a new plan," said Max. "We're headed to Kentucky."

"Kentucky?" said Georgia.

Max explained about the school report that Chad had been clutching in his hand, as well as the deed to the house.

"There's no one around there," said Max. "And we can head southeast and avoid the whole mess of Ohio, which is fairly densely populated."

"But we don't have any maps," said Georgia. "Unless you found some, that is. How are we going to get there?"

"We didn't find any maps," said Max. "Maybe we can find some at a gas station or something. Or a truck stop. But either way, all we have to do is use the compass and head southeast. If we cross over Route 64, then we've gone too far south, and we'll have to keep going east."

"How do you know that?"

Max shrugged. "Just some fact that stuck in my head, I guess. I used to have to process interstate roads sometimes at work."

"All right," said Georgia. "Let's do it."

She didn't have to think about it long, noticed Mandy. She, like the others, trusted Max.

But what was going to happen when he eventually made a mistake? He was only human, after all.

"I'll take the Honda," said Max.

"I'll go with you," said Mandy.

Max shook his head. "I need you with Georgia. I'll take Chad and keep an eye on him. James, you can come with us. That OK, Georgia?"

"Sure," said Georgia. "I know he'll be just as safe with you as with me, Max."

Max nodded. "Well, let's not waste any more time. I'll

lead the way. You follow, Georgia. If there's a hiccup, we'll just have to improvise."

6

JOHN

"I know you're out there," shouted someone. The man sounded middle-aged. But that was just a guess.

John didn't dare to even whisper. He just hoped that the others would have enough sense to stay still, and not say anything. And that Cynthia would keep her gun ready.

Footsteps through the woods. Heavy ones.

The man would be there soon enough. He was crashing through the woods, breaking small branches as he moved.

John glanced at Cynthia. She looked scared. But she looked ready. She was holding her gun with both hands. Maybe she didn't have the right technique. Not that John knew what the right way to hold a handgun was. She was pointing it forward. He supposed that was the most important thing.

Nothing could be perfect. Not the way things were, not since the EMP had hit and society had collapsed.

"I saw your setup at the farmhouse," shouted the man. "Come on out. I'm a friend. My name's Miller. I was just at the farmhouse, looking for the bastards who attacked my family. Come on out. My name's Miller. I don't know who you are."

John still didn't move. He suspected the worst. He suspected a trick.

If the man came into view, John was ready to shoot. He was ready to kill.

Something about the whole situation felt different than when he'd run across John and Sara such a short time ago. They hadn't had that threatening vibe around them.

But this man who he couldn't see—he spoke like he was mad. Like he was angry, enraged. And he'd moved harshly through the woods, as if he was looking or a fight.

"I don't know if you know Max," said the man who called himself Miller. "He was at the farmhouse before you."

Max? Did this guy know John's brother?

"Whoever you are," said Miller, speaking loudly. "I know you're not the men who killed my wife and son. I saw that you buried the bodies. I saw your journals. You're normal people, like me. Well, as normal as we can be."

"You know Max?" said John, speaking for the first time.

"Yeah," said Miller. "Who are you? Show yourself to me."

John might have been acting stupidly. But curiosity got the better of him. He wanted to know more about what had happened to his brother.

John stood up.

"What are you doing?" hissed Cynthia.

"Dude," whispered Derek. "Don't go."

John ignored them and walked forward, through the thick trees.

Moments later, he saw the man named Miller.

John was almost surprised that Miller didn't simply shoot him, that it wasn't a trick.

But Miller made no move for the gun in its holster on his belt.

"I'm John."

"Miller," said Miller.

Miller was wearing clothes that had been torn in places. There was blood all over his shirt, dark and dried. It didn't seem to be his blood. He stood tall and strong, like he hadn't been injured.

Everything in the way he stood screamed: anger.

"Max is my brother," said John.

Miller's face lightened a little. Not much, though. There was too much anger there.

"As I told your brother," said Miller. "I knew your grandfather. Good man. Good family."

"What happened to Max?"

"He left. They were coming. I stayed to fight and defend my property and my family. Dumbest damn thing I've ever done."

"You lost your wife and son?"

Miller couldn't even get the words to come out. He just nodded. There was pain in his eyes. Deep pain that would never go away.

Miller didn't seem like a threat. At least not to John and the party.

"Come on, everyone," called out John. "You can come out. He's not going to hurt us."

Slowly, Cynthia, Derek, and Sara emerged through the trees.

Miller nodded at all of them.

"We need to exchange some information," said Miller. His face was deadly serious. "I need to know about the men who attacked us. I need my revenge."

John nodded. He felt bad about what he was going to say next, but he knew he had to say it. The whole world had gone to shit, and this wasn't the time for altruism, even if the man had lost his family. "That's fine. But I'm going to need something in return. We're barely surviving as it is."

Miller studied him. "Fine," he said. "Whatever you need."

"Let's head back to the farmhouse," said John. "We can talk there."

"Good," said Miller. "You have a vehicle?"

John shook his head.

"Come in mine, then."

The others seemed a little hesitant, but they seemed to trust John's instincts. They all followed Miller back to his SUV and got in.

"You know where it is then?" said John.

Miller nodded. He was already driving fast down the rural road.

To say that Miller wasn't in the mood for small talk would have been an understatement.

But what could you expect from a man who'd just lost his wife and kid?

John didn't know what to say. But maybe it was better that way. He knew there was nothing he could say to make it better. The fact was that things wouldn't get better. This was the new reality. The new world.

Miller pulled into the driveway, driving fast, dirt and

gravel from the driveway spraying up. He stopped hard right at the front of the farmhouse.

They got out wordlessly. Miller didn't wait for them. He walked right up to the front door and walked inside.

"Maybe I can find us something to eat," said Cynthia.

John nodded at her, and she started going through the piles of food stores, passing things around to everyone.

Food usually brightened everyone's spirits. But not in this case.

There was going to be no quenching Miller's rage. No calming him down. Anyone could have seen it just in the way he sat, all hunched up, tense. And from his face.

John watched as Miller ate one of the energy bars Cynthia had timidly handed him. He wasn't doing it for enjoyment. It was purely fuel for him. Fuel for his quest to find those who'd done it.

"So what do you know?" said Miller. "Tell me everything."

"We..." started John. He realized that he didn't know any more than Miller did. He'd already told him about the bodies in the farmhouse. "Truth is, Miller, I don't really know much. We just met Derek and Susan... sorry, I mean Sara here. They were telling us about what's happened in the suburbs. A sort of rogue militia has taken over." John looked over to Derek and Sara, hoping they'd start to fill in the gaps.

"Yeah," said Derek. "I could go on and on, but the gist of it is that we had to get out."

"Tell me more," said Miller, his eyes narrowing.

Derek told him everything he'd just told John. Sara chimed in here and there, but Derek did most of the talking.

When he was finally done, Miller didn't say anything.

"You think it was the same guys?" said John, looking at Miller.

Miller gave a stiff nod. "Definitely."

"But what about all those bodies we found here in the farmhouse?"

Miller shook his head. "These guys were professionals. They knew how to fight, most of them anyway. The others were just cruel and savage. They were taking orders. Doesn't sound like the group here. After all, they just ended up killing each other."

"How can you be sure, though?" said Cynthia.

John knew her well enough now to know that she thought she could convince Miller that there wasn't a fight to fight anymore. She thought that somehow she could save him if she "fixed" him psychologically. But John knew that there wasn't a fix. He could see it in Miller's eyes. Miller would go down fighting. John had never been more sure of anything in his life.

"I dug up some of the bodies," said Miller. "Didn't take long. Shallow graves."

Cynthia shuddered at the thought.

The truth was, they hadn't even really "buried" the bodies at all. Shallow graves was an exaggeration.

Miller was silent for a while. No one else dared to speak. Not with the intensity he was emanating.

"I'm going to get them," he said finally. "Maybe not the same bastards who did it. But I'm going to destroy them from the inside out. I'll go after the leader. That's what I'll do."

"But," said John. "It's... the whole thing is set up just like a government at this point. I don't know how it happened so fast. But that's the truth. I think part of it is that the prison gangs already had their hierarchies. And that just sort of continued once they gained control of the whole Main Line area."

"I don't care," said Miller. "I've got to try. I'm going back there. Tell me more. I need details. I need to know how to find this bastard Kor or whatever he calls himself."

"I... I don't know," said Derek, looing nervous as Miller bore down on him with his gaze. "It'd probably be really hard to track him down. I think they keep moving. He keeps his inner circle tight, and there's some kind of crazy complicated chain of command."

"You were telling me," said John, "that Kor was after this shielded shortwave radio, right?"

"Yeah," said Derek. "One shielded with a Faraday cage. That's the main thing he's after."

"A shortwave radio shielded with Faraday cage?" mused Miller, rubbing his chin.

For the first time since John had met him, Miller looked almost... happy. Well, you couldn't call it happy really. But there was a smile on his face. A horrible kind of smile. The kind of smile that a man has when he knows he can get what he wants, but when what he wants isn't a good thing.

"You've got a plan?" said John.

"If that's what he wants," said Miller. "Then that's what he's going to get."

"You have a radio?" said John. His mind instantly went to a thousand places. If he had the radio, maybe they could use it themselves to communicate with whoever else was out there with the same device. If there really was anyone.

"No," said Miller, smirking. "But I'll pretend that I have one. I'll get close to him and take him out. And whoever else I can in the process."

John nodded silently.

"When are you leaving?"

"Now," said Miller. "I have a small box that I'll say is the radio. I won't let anyone look at it but Kor himself, the mighty leader of the shit-eating monsters who took my family from me. It'll get me close to him."

"Won't they just take it from you?" said John. "Why would they bring you to him?"

Miller paused. "You're a smart man," he said. "I'll tell them that I'll reveal the location only to their leader. That'll get me a meeting with him. If there's one thing I know it's that you can get what you want by giving a man what he wants. And he wants this, right?" He looked at Derek and Sara, drilling into them again with his fierce angry eyes.

"Sounds like it," said Derek.

"More than anything," said Sara. "He's sending raiding crews all over, looking for it."

"Good," said Miller. "Now I'm a man of my word. You've helped me. What can I do for you?"

He stared right at John.

"Tell me about Max," said John.

"He's gone west," said Miller. "He and his group. There were... I don't know, six of them with him?"

"Six?" said John.

Who could they have been? One was Chad, which didn't make any sense.

"Fine people," said Miller. "They were the last ones aside from me to see my wife and son..."

Miller looked like he was about to start tearing up. But he didn't. He had no more tears left to give.

"Any idea where they were headed exactly?" said John.

Miller shrugged. "I don't think they knew. They knew, though, that they couldn't defend the farmhouse."

"They couldn't?"

Miller shook his head. "And they were right to leave. Look at what happened to me. In my hubris, I thought I could defend my house. I had everything set up perfectly. I thought I was so clever, and look what it got me. Max did the right thing. He took them all away. Where they ended up, I haven't the slightest clue. And whether they got there safely, I have even less of an idea of that."

It was tough news to swallow. John had been hoping that Miller could have given him something more specific.

It also meant that John and Cynthia were likely going to have to abandon the farmhouse. Max would have been better prepared. He knew more about this sort of thing than John. If Max couldn't do it, with his small army of six people, then what chance did John and Cynthia have? Even if their new acquaintances Derek and Sara stayed along with them?

Not much of a chance at all.

"Well," said Miller gruffly, getting up. "I'm going."

For a moment, John didn't know what to say. His mind was reeling. Headed in a hundred directions at once.

"Good luck, Miller," said John.

Miller walked out the front door, letting the screen door slam behind him.

"How could you let him go like that?" hissed Cynthia. "He's marching to his death."

"What did you want me to do?"

"You could have not told him about the shortwave radio, for one thing. Now he has a plan."

"They're going to kill him," muttered Sara, covering her face in her hands.

"Who are we to tell him what to do?" said John. "He lost his family. This is what he wants to do. He's not going to be happy until he gets his revenge."

"You're just saying all that 'a man's got to do what a man's got to do' stuff," said Sara.

John shrugged. "Sometimes that's the truth."

"He made it sound dangerous here," said Sara. "Like people are going to be coming back."

John nodded. "Yeah," he said. "And it sounded like my brother knew he wasn't able to defend this place. And that was with more people. Even if you two stayed. I was hoping I'd be able to convince you to stay. Strength in numbers and all that. But now, frankly, I wouldn't recommend it."

"Yeah," said Derek. "I don't think it'd be a good idea if we stayed."

"Can't blame you for that," said John. "I think we should be leaving ourselves. What do you say, Cynthia?"

"I don't think we should stay," said Cynthia, sighing as she looked around the relative comfort of the living room. "But this place has started to really feel like home. I hate to leave it. And where would we go?"

"West," said John. "Where else? Follow my brother. What do you say, Derek and Sarah? Want to join us? There's strength in numbers, even out on the road."

Derek and Sara looked at each other. They were one of those couples that could communicate with a single glance.

They both looked back at John and nodded together.

"We'll come," said Derek. "But we don't know for how long."

"And we know some trails that might be helpful," said Sara.

"Good, we'll start the preparations now. We'll leave tonight. As soon as we can."

"Tonight?" said Cynthia. "Why not tomorrow morning? Early."

"Who knows when they'll come," said John. "We might already be too late."

7

MILLER

Miller was barreling down the dirt road in his SUV. He must have been going at least 80 MPH.

There was a turn up ahead. A tough curve, even at slower speeds.

He didn't slow down. He was too intent on getting there, on exacting his revenge, that he could barely wait. He could barely contain himself. He was going to make his life worth something. He was going to do what he had to do.

He took the turn too hard. Too fast.

The SUV skidded to the side. Miller lost control. The rear tires lost traction, sliding sideways, the rear of the vehicle veering across the asphalt.

"Shit," shouted Miller as he pulled on the wheel hard, trying to regain control.

Frantic images flashed through his mind, images of his immediate future. He saw himself lying on the side of the road, bleeding from his injuries. He no longer cared about himself or his well being. Certainly not his health.

As far as he was concerned, his life was no more.

But his purpose. His goal.

If he couldn't do it, if he couldn't kill this man Kor. If he couldn't make them pay, then it was all for nothing.

At the last moment, Miller regained control of the SUV. He didn't look behind him. He didn't know how close he'd come to slamming into a tree. He didn't want to know. All he wanted to do was continue forward. Complete his mission. Kill Kor. And whoever else he could.

Miller forced himself to slow down as he headed south. He knew that it was better to go slow and steady. For now.

He glanced over at the passenger seat. Normally, his wife would have sat there. In her place, there was no one. But there were guns. A couple handguns, and an AR-15.

There was no way they'd let Miller near the leader while carrying an AR-15. And they'd surely pat him down for handguns, knives, and explosives. For any weapons whatsoever.

Miller would have to think carefully about his plan. That was going to be tough. Right now he was so full of rage that he just wanted to rush in, guns blazing.

If he wanted to achieve his goal, he'd have to slow down and plot carefully. He'd have to use every fiber of his intelligence, marshaling all his cunning.

Maybe he could meet Kor, the leader, take careful note of the location, and then sneak back later to exact his revenge. No, that wouldn't work. They'd probably blindfold Miller. If they had any sense at all. And unfortunately it sounded like they did.

Maybe Miller could booby-trap himself with a hidden

explosive, and then detonate himself, destroying everything around him.

Miller wasn't keen on that idea. It stank of cowardice. Sure, it was self-sacrificing, and he was fine with that. He didn't expect to live through what he'd go through. But he wanted to be aware of every moment of it. An explosion would kill him first. He wouldn't get the satisfaction of seeing the leader die in front of him, at his own hand.

The sky was full of gray clouds. Some of the trees were starting to lose their leaves. It was happening early this year. Some had already lost their leaves. Early bloomers, Miller's family had always called them. They'd never known the technical name.

Miller's thoughts turned towards his family.

He'd been proud of his son. He'd been becoming quite a good shot with a rifle. And he was learning all the things one needed to know to run a self-sufficient homestead. He'd been scared, like everyone else, but for a boy of such a young age, he'd done a remarkable job of continuing on, of doing what had to be done. He'd even been a source of comfort for Miller's wife, who'd had the most trouble out of all of them adjusting to the post-EMP world.

No matter how hard he tried, Miller couldn't shake the image of his wife and son lying dead on the ground. They'd taken multiple bullets each. They'd been killed instantly, most likely. There hadn't been anything to do for them. No amount of first aid, no matter how expertly applied, would have done anything for them. Their eyes had simply stared straight ahead, blank and lifeless.

Miller and his family had fought hard. Max and his group had just left the house. The drawbridge had been up, and Miller and his wife and son had shot at the enemies from their home windows. They'd stayed out of view as much as they could.

Miller himself had taken the most risks. He'd exposed his body the most, trying to get off as many good shots as he could. He'd killed many of them. But not enough.

It wasn't fair that he was still alive. He should have been the one to die. His son had had many years of life ahead of him.

Miller's face felt hot and red. He doubted the anger would ever leave him.

And that was the way he wanted it.

Up ahead, the road transitioned from dirt to pavement.

The tires rolled smoothly over the pavement. There was no longer the noise of the SUV moving over the dirt road. No noise from the bumps, from the potholes.

Miller didn't like the quiet. Not now. He wanted things to be noisy. It helped him with his thoughts.

At any moment, Miller might run into a group. Most likely a militia group.

The ones that he'd fought were likely long gone. Miller had killed half of them anyway.

He didn't yet have a plan, and he needed more time to think.

It was a mental battle. He wanted to simply rush ahead into the fray, ready to die in the fight. But he knew he needed a plan.

It was tough, but Miller slowed the SUV down and pulled over to the side of the road. He sat there with the vehicle running.

He wouldn't have said that it felt like his world was crashing down around him. Because it already had.

Everything about his existence felt different. Everything he looked at seemed darker. More intense.

He was a different man than he had been.

Gazing through the windshield, he was in a fog.

Up ahead, there was a flash of metal down the road. Something glinted in the dull light from the clouded sky.

It was a pickup truck, barreling down the road at top speed. It was headed straight towards Miller.

As it got closer, he saw that there were men in the bed of the pickup. Three or four of them. It was hard to tell.

Despite Miller thinking he'd been ready, he did nothing. He just sat there as the pickup sped towards him.

The pickup sped past Miller's SUV. For a moment, it seemed like they'd just drive right on past.

Miller cursed himself for letting an opportunity like that fly by.

There was no doubt in his mind that they were part of the same organization that had attacked his home. He'd let an opportunity for revenge slip by.

Even if it wasn't the leader, Kor, it was something.

Miller slammed his fist into the dash so hard that he left a dent. Pain flared in his hand.

Miller's eye followed the pickup in his rearview mirror.

The driver suddenly slammed on the brakes, sending the pickup into a fishtailing skid.

The pickup was maybe 200 feet behind Miller. The men in the bed jumped down onto the road. They all held guns. Assault rifles. One had a shotgun. Probably automatic.

One wore full military fatigues and a combat helmet. But he didn't walk like the military guys did. He was probably some lowlife from prison who'd stolen the uniform.

There were three of them. No, four.

Miller's mind was having trouble taking it all in.

Miller reached for the gun in his holster. He did it automatically.

The rage inside him was telling him to fight. To kill as many as he could.

But his brain was telling him that this was his chance. He shouldn't fight them. He should convince them to take him to Kor, their leader. Only then could Miller find his true purpose, his revenge.

8

JAMES

"You feeling OK, Max?" said James, studying Max's bruised and battered face.

"I'm fine," said Max.

They were driving down the highway. They'd left the ghost town of Albion, heading south.

The toll booth gates had been up, the toll booths abandoned. There wasn't another car on the highway. Not a single soul in sight.

The plan, as Max had explained it, was to stay in Pennsylvania, cutting straight down until they hit West Virginia. From there, they'd make their way to Kentucky.

"You sure you don't want me to drive?" said James.

Max shook his head. "Maybe later," he said.

"I can drive, you know."

"I know," said Max. "But let's stick with this plan for now. OK?"

"Sure, Max," said James.

James still couldn't believe what Max had done for them all. It wasn't just Max, though. It was his mom.

His mom had always seemed like a strong woman. James had never admitted it to her, but he'd looked up to her. That was before the EMP, when they were living their normal lives in the suburbs.

James hadn't known his dad. Not much, at least. A few visits here and there, scattered throughout the years. James couldn't even picture his face now. Not that he tried much.

But James had never realized just how strong his mom was. Just how much she could go through...

"How's Chad doing?" said Max.

James glanced at Chad in the backseat.

"I can hear you, you know," said Chad. "I'm fine."

He didn't look fine. He still looked dazed. But his face was starting to look more normal. That goofy expression was mostly gone.

"We thought we'd lost you," said Max. "What the hell happened back there?"

"Dunno," mumbled Chad. "Must have been the stress or something. Sorry. I screwed up. It won't happen again."

Max didn't say anything.

"Maybe it's better if you talk about it," said James. "I had to go to the school counselor a couple times. I was getting into fights at school. I didn't think it would do anything, but talking about what was going on really helped me."

"He doesn't need to talk about it," said Max. "We're all going through it. There's nothing to discuss."

"Yeah," said Chad. "I'm fine. It's just... everything, you know?"

"No need to go on," said Max.

They drove in silence for a while. The sky was a dark

gray. James wished that the sun would come out. Everything seemed so much grimmer when the sun wasn't shining.

James spent a lot of time looking in the side mirror. Most of the time, he could see the Ford Bronco behind them. He couldn't see his mother's face, or Sadie's, but he knew they were there, and it made him feel better. He was worried about them, especially Sadie, who still was having trouble adapting to the harsh new reality of a post-EMP world.

"They're fine, James," said Max, glancing over and seeing that James was watching them in the mirror. "There's no need to worry about them. Not any more than normal, I mean."

"Maybe I should have gone in the car with them," said James. "If something happens..."

"I need you here with me," said Max. "And don't worry. Your mom and Mandy can handle anything. Mandy's getting to be a good shot."

James nodded. "Better than me, I think."

"No shame in that," said Max. "Just keep practicing."

"How can I practice? It's not like there's any time."

"A lot of it's mental," said Max. "You've got to keep yourself in control, no matter what the situation. You'll shoot a lot better if you've got your shit together, if you can stay calm. Reasonably calm, I mean."

"So we're going to take the highway all the way down?" said James, changing the subject. He didn't like talking about his weaknesses, not in front of Max.

In a way, it was almost as if Max was becoming a father figure to him. Not that he'd ever tell Max that.

"Yeah," said Max. "It might expose us more, but we'll

make better time. Better than trying to figure out all those side roads. We'd end up getting lost again and running into more trouble."

"Makes sense," said James. "The car seems like it's working OK."

"Yeah," said Max. "If I keep the revs under 5,000, the turbo doesn't kick in. That helps save gas."

"I always wanted a car like this," said James. "But now that I'm in it... I don't know, it seems a little silly. Especially given the situation."

"Yeah," said Max. "Not really the most practical. I bet it was good on the track. But we're not on the track now."

"Sounds like a variation of 'we're not in Kansas anymore,'" said James.

"That's for sure," said Max.

They all fell silent for a while.

So far, they hadn't seen another vehicle on the highway.

They drove by billboards, advertisements for products that would likely never be in production again. They were reminders of a world that was lost. Lost for good.

They drove under the automated sensors that registered the electronic alternatives to paying tolls as they went. Not that those did anything anymore.

"Let's just hope the gates are up at the toll booths," said Max.

"What do we do if they aren't?"

"We can move them," said Max. "But I just don't want to waste time. And every time we stop, we put ourselves in more danger."

"There's one up ahead."

"Your eyes are sharper than mine. Good catch."

It was a strange sight, seeing the toll booth again.

They were empty, and the gates were down this time.

"Looks like we're going to have to stop," said Max. "I'll get out and see if I can lift it. It's business as usual—keep your gun ready. You'd better get out, James. That rifle won't be much good if you stay in the car."

The rifle had been leaning against James's knee. He'd almost forgotten it was there. It had become a part of him since the EMP. It rarely left his side. Max had been good about drilling that into their heads.

Max slowed to a stop.

Behind them, Georgia stopped the Bronco as well.

Max signaled for them to stay in the car.

He and James got out.

The air was a little warmer than it had been. But the sky was still a dark gray. Rock cliffs, artificially created, lined the sides of the highway.

It was strange, standing in the middle of an abandoned interstate.

"You see anyone? Anything?" said Max.

Max was using his binoculars to scan the area, while staying crouched off to the side of the Honda. James imitated him, keeping low and using the car as cover.

"Nothing," said James.

"Hey," said Chad, opening the back door. "What the hell's going on?"

He must have still been pretty out of it if he hadn't heard the whole plan.

"Back in the car, Chad," said Max.

Chad stayed in the car, but kept the door open. It was stupid of him, abandoning the potential protection of the car door, but there wasn't time to babysit him and tell him what to do. James didn't feel like it was his job anyway.

Chad was a grown man, even if he was suffering from some kind of shock.

"I don't see anything either," said Max, letting the binoculars drop down to where they hung around his neck.

James watched Max as Max went to move the gate. James knew that he had to keep his eyes on his surroundings, rather than watching Max.

"Shit," muttered Max. "I can't get it. Come over here and help me, James."

"Should I get my mom and the others to cover us?"

"Let's just get this over with," said Max.

James had to set his rifle down to help Max. The gate was hard to move. James tested it by pulling up on it. Maybe they'd' be able to move it if they both used all their strength.

"We could just drive through it," said James. "It's pretty flimsy."

"We might damage the car," said Max. "Come on. Give it your all."

James settled into a good stance, keeping his back straight.

"Go," said Max.

They both pulled up, as hard as they could. Slowly, they got the gate to start moving. Once they got it past a certain point, the gears seemed to loosen up.

"OK," said Max. "I can take it from here."

Max was taller than James, and was able to push the gate almost all the way to its normal open position.

James quickly grabbed his rifle from the ground, and made sure to look around.

Still, there was no one.

"Do you hear that?" said James, looking down the highway.

Max shook his head. "What do you hear?"

"Sounds like an engine. I don't know. It's something."

James stared down the long empty stretch of gray highway, looking past and through the toll booth.

"I don't see anything," said Max.

"Me neither," said James.

"Come on," said Max. "We'd better get out of here. I hear it now."

The sound was getting louder. It was definitely the engine of some vehicle. Aside from the Ford Bronco behind them, and their own Honda, there was hardly another noise for what seemed like miles around. The silence made the isolated noise seem eerie and ominous.

"But we're going to be heading right towards the noise," said James.

Max nodded. He looked like he was thinking.

"Everything OK?" called out James's mom, leaning out the window of the beat-up Ford Bronco.

"There's someone coming."

There weren't any options, in terms of where to go. There were guardrails on the side of the highway, and there wasn't anywhere to drive anyway. If they were going to drive, it was either go forward, towards the noise, or turn around and hope to outrun whoever it was.

The only other option was to abandon the vehicles and hike on out. James knew that that option meant leaving behind all the gear. Not to mention the vehicles.

James's heart was beating fast. He was nervous, and worried about not only himself, but his family. It was times like these that he was glad he wasn't the one making the decisions. If it'd been left up to him, he might have panicked and had everyone run into the woods, only to pay for the decision later.

"We've got to keep going," said Max. His expression was hard to read. "Come on, quick. Back in the car."

"What's going on?" said Chad, sounding sleepy, as Max and James piled back into the car.

James's rifle didn't leave his hand. The solid feel of it made him feel a little better. But not much.

No one answered Chad. If he was so out of it that he hadn't figured out what was going on, then that was his own problem.

"No one's going to tell me?" said Chad.

"Just keep your gun ready," said Max, putting the Honda into first gear.

James was practically holding his breath as they drove through the now open toll gate.

"I can't hear anything now," said James. Max was picking up speed. The Honda's movement drowned out the faint noise.

"Hopefully we'll just drive by them," said Max. "Whoever they are."

"I'm ready to fight," said James. "I'll do whatever it takes. You can count on me, Max."

As he said the words, though, they felt hollow. Sure, they were true. He'd do whatever it took, especially when he thought about his mom and sister. But he felt anything but courageous. His body felt cold and empty, and he wondered if he'd have the strength to fight.

"Just stay ready," said Max. "Another fight is the last thing we need. We'll avoid it if we can."

"Hey man," said Chad, from the backseat. "Not everyone's bad, you know? Not everyone's out to get us. Why do you guys think it's always about a fight? Maybe whoever it is is just like us, just looking to survive."

That was probably the most Chad had spoken in the last day.

"Get your rifle ready, Chad," said Max.

9

JOHN

The sun had gone down. It wasn't missed. John welcomed the darkness, knowing that it would provide them the cover they'd need to escape the area.

He didn't know who would come or how soon they'd come, but he knew that the sooner they got out, the better.

They'd spent the last few hours preparing, getting as ready as they could.

Derek and Sara were already pretty loaded down. They'd started off with a lot of food, and there wasn't much room left in their packs. Since no one knew what lay ahead, and whether the two "couples" would split up or continue together, they couldn't let Derek and Sara take all the cooking gear, for instance. John and Cynthia weren't exactly a couple, even though they were starting to act like that, with their own way of speaking, and their own special way of getting on each other's nerves.

But nothing could be perfect, and concessions were made. The main thing was that they packed weapons instead of other useful things. There were so many guns that they had their pick. They each took two handguns and some sort of rifle. They took as much ammo as they could, making sure that they had what matched their gun. Sara was a great deal of help with that aspect of things.

Most of their packs were loaded down with food and water. Derek and Sara cautioned them on how much water they'd need. They couldn't guarantee they'd find a water source along the way, even with their purification tablets and devices.

John was already well aware of the water situation. It had been difficult for himself and Cynthia when they'd hiked out from the suburbs. But this journey would likely be far, far longer.

They didn't know where to go. The only idea they had was to head west. West was where Max had gone, to lesser populated areas.

John didn't hold any illusions that he'd somehow run into Max along the way. The chances were simply too slim. It was better not to hold out any hope. And what difference would it make, anyway?

Sure, seeing family would be comforting, during these intense and trying times, but John reminded himself that he and Max hadn't been close. It was better to simply focus on forging new relationships, new bonds. Everything had changed, and everyone John had known was likely dead, or about to die. It was better to be pragmatic about the future. New alliances and friends—that was the way to survive. Better than clinging to something that hadn't ever really been there in the first place. Or to delusional hopes of reconnection.

Not many words were spoken as they prepared. There wasn't much to say, except exchange ideas on packing, and on what needed to be taken.

Finally, they were ready. None of the four of them needed to announce it. It simply became obvious. The four of them shouldered their packs in silence.

They were ready to leave.

John was lost in his own thoughts for a moment. He turned towards his new companions. He barely knew them, yet he was setting out on a life and death trek across now-unknown lands.

At the very least, they seemed practical-minded. And not overly prone to chitchat. And they seemed like honest people. Not to mention worried and scared. Which was good. They weren't clueless. They understood the dangers as well as anyone could.

John's mind occasionally flashed back to the horrors he'd seen in the cities. And to the people he'd seen die in front of him. Their names escaped him now, maybe as a type of defense mechanism. But the images were clean and crisp, burned into his memory.

Cynthia was the first to break the silence that hung between them all.

"Should we do anything to the house?" she said. "Like lock it up?"

It seemed like such a pedestrian worry that John laughed. He hadn't thought about doing anything with the house except for simply leaving it. Worrying about locking it up, or turning off the gas—those were all pre-EMP worries.

"You're laughing at me?" said Cynthia, but there was laugher in her voice and a smile on her face.

Pretty soon, they were all laughing.

The tension was broken, along with the silence.

And it wasn't even that funny of a joke.

"Maybe we'd better call the post office and tell them to hold the mail," said Sara.

That made them all laugh even harder.

"And I'll call the paper and tell them not to deliver," said Derek, chiming in.

John laughed so hard that his stomach ached.

John hadn't even realized how much tension he and the others had all been holding onto. Now that it was broken, he felt a little better. A little warmer. A little lighter.

He felt like he was traveling with good people. Something could come of this. He felt optimistic, a little hopeful. Even though he knew he shouldn't have.

So far, he'd been lucky. And he knew it.

He'd been unprepared. There wasn't a reason that he should have survive. Neither he nor Cynthia deserved it. Maybe Derek and Sara didn't either. John didn't know, and he wasn't going to make that judgment.

John had cheated death. There were probably others who'd done the same. Statistically, there were bound to be people who'd survived, even when the odds were against them.

In all likelihood, most would die. Like John had seen in the cities. The majority of those who'd survive, long-term, would be those who'd been prepared. In some fashion, whether it was gear or simply a good plan. They'd know what to do. And how to act. Right when it happened.

The faster someone responded, the more likely they were to have gotten out, to have survived. John had waited too long, holing himself up for two weeks in his apartment. He'd been unbelievably lucky.

So far.

Long-term survival was different than just getting out. It meant having more than a plan and gear. It meant finding the right environment.

Most of all, it meant having a certain attitude. Gear, of course, was required. But the attitude, that drive to survive, to keep going, that was what would separate the survivors from the less fortunate.

And luck.

So far, John had been able to dive deep inside himself and marshal resources he'd never known existed. It'd been as much an internal struggle as an external one.

He knew he had it now. But the others? That was perhaps John's reservation about them. Derek and Sara were good people, but did they have that drive? Did Cynthia? John wasn't sure. And that worried him.

"Well," said John. "Let's head out. We'll try to find that trail you two told us about."

"Sounds good," said Derek. "Should just be a couple miles down the road."

They set off, leaving through the back door of the farmhouse. John turned his head only once to look, to say goodbye to the place that, truthfully, held no sentimental value for him whatsoever. The only thing the farmhouse had meant to him, before the EMP, was bitterness that Max had inherited it and not himself.

The moon was out, which made walking at night easier. They had flashlights with them and plenty of batteries, for when the moon was covered by clouds, or when it was a mere sliver in the dark sky. The batteries, like everything else, had come from the packs of the dead men in the farmhouse.

John's only concern with the flashlights was that the lights would give them away. It'd be better to let their eyes adapt to the darkness and make their way as best they could.

They hadn't discussed it as a group, but John was planning on traveling exclusively at night. That had worked for him and Cynthia on their way out of the suburbs. And he hoped it would work for them again.

It didn't take them long to cross the field. Under the cover of the trees, it was darker.

Derek led the way. He'd said he knew a shortcut, a path that would take them a little ways down the road. Then they'd take the road to the next trail.

John followed Derek close enough to talk to him. Cynthia and Sara followed.

"If we can find a vehicle somewhere," said John. "It'll make this all a lot easier."

"Only problem," said Derek, "is we don't know where we're going."

"Well, it'll help us get to hopefully safer areas faster," said John.

"I think it's better if we stick with the trails," said Derek.

Sara nodded her agreement.

"We can stay hidden on the trails," said Derek. "I'm hoping we can avoid using these guns."

"You don't think there'll be others at some point?" said John. "Others with the same ideas?"

"Well," said Derek. "Hikers are good people. I mean, when we did the Long Trail, we met so many great people. Great friends. I hope they're OK now."

"They may have been good people then," said John, "but the EMP changed everything. Everything is different. You've got to realize that. People will do whatever they have to do."

"People stay the same," said Derek. "They're either good or bad."

John didn't say anything. He didn't want to waste his energy arguing, but he was becoming quickly concerned that Derek saw things in an unrealistic black and white way. Derek seemed to think that good people never did bad things. Hadn't he seen what had happened in the suburbs? Or at least heard about it? He'd been the one to tell him the rumors about the militia leader, Kor.

But for Derek, it seemed that Kor was bad because he was already a bad person. Derek wasn't considering the good people who'd likely joined up in the militia and then gone on to do bad things, simply because it was easier. Sure, some of them may have been deluded into thinking they were recreating a new world, a new system of order.

What would happen when they came across someone who was ready to do whatever it took to survive? John didn't think he could count on Derek. In fact, he didn't know if he could count on any of them.

And that wasn't a good feeling.

10

MILLER

Miller was breathing hard. His hand clutched his handgun.

Should he fight or try to execute his plan?

He still hadn't worked out that plan that he'd been thinking about. There were a lot of complications. A lot of problems with it.

He glanced in the mirror. They were getting close.

Three of them. No, four. Maybe five. He wasn't sure. It was hard to tell. Nothing was ever clear in a situation like that.

Miller took a deep breath, focusing on his breathing. He let himself have one slow, controlled inhale and one slow, controlled exhale.

Miller was smart enough to know that in a situation like this, the mind was the best weapon any man had at his disposal. The guns and the knives and the fists—these were just dumb implements. Sure, they were helpful. Necessary, even.

But the mind. It was the most dangerous of them all.

Miller got himself under control.

He rolled down his window.

He stuck out his arm and gave a casual wave.

"How's it going, boys?"

One of them was right up at his window. He looked mean. He had a big red beard, bushy and untamed. Wild looking. There was the glint of violence in his eyes.

"Identify yourself."

He pointed the muzzle of his assault rifle right at Miller.

Miller wasn't scared. Not for his own safety. They only thing he feared was not being able to carry out his plan.

"Miller. Just Miller. That's what they call me." He tried to make his words sound as casual as he could.

"What are you doing here?"

"Doing what anyone's doing," said Miller. "Just surviving. Just hanging on."

Miller kept a smile fixed to his face.

The red-bearded man glared at him. His buddies stood behind him, their guns ready.

"What are you boys doing out here?" said Miller, playing innocent. "I thought the military wasn't... you know... wasn't exactly operational since the EMP."

No answer.

"I was having a problem, maybe you guys could help me out."

Still no answer.

The orange-bearded man was peering past Miller into the SUV, eyeing the guns. He was looking for supplies, looking for gear.

Maybe he was looking for a Faraday-shielded shortwave radio.

But who carried one of those around?

The trick was just to casually slip it into the conversation.

"What have you got there? The firearms."

"Oh, those? Just some of my old hunting gear. You know, you've got to be prepared when you're out here."

"Out of the car." The words came out of him cold and calculated. No sympathy in them.

"Hey," said Miller. "That's fine. But come on, don't take my guns from me. How the hell am I going to survive out here? There are some nasty types around, you know."

"Not my problem. Out of the car."

"You got it, bud," said Miller.

Miller got out of the car, keeping his hands where the militia guys could see them.

Inside, Miller was raging. He wanted to tear out all their throats. Maybe eat their hearts. Some of that crazy movie shit. Exacting his revenge and all that.

But outside, he remained calm. He couldn't give himself away.

Fake it, he kept telling himself. Fake it until the revenge. It'll be sweeter than all this bullshit.

Miller stood off to the side. One of the others, a guy with a shotgun and a particularly grungy look, stood by him. He jammed the butt of his shotgun into Miller's stomach for no good reason whatsoever.

Miller bent over in pain.

He wanted to elbow the idiot in the face, take the shotgun, and blast through the guts of them all.

But he kept calm.

"That hurt, buddy," he said, keeping that idiotic smile on his face.

Keep it there, no matter what, he told himself over and over.

The other three militia men were all over the SUV, rooting through the guns and the gear. They were talking to themselves over their findings.

And they had good reason to be. After all, Miller had some good stuff with him.

He didn't give a shit about his stuff.

There was a time when Miller had polished his guns, kept them looking pretty. A time when he'd kept his knives razor sharp. A time when gear had meant so much to him.

Now they were just objects. Cold and utilitarian.

They were nothing compared to his wife and son, mutilated by bullets and buried by none other than Miller himself, right there on the property they'd lived their entire lives on.

The three weren't paying any attention to Miller.

"What do we do with him?" said Miller's guard, shoving the shotgun muzzle further against Miller's flesh.

"Kill him," said the orange-bearded man. He said it casually, not even looking at Miller.

"Sorry, buddy," said the guy with the shotgun, looking Miller in the eyes for the first time.

But there wasn't any apology in his eyes. He wasn't bothered by killing. He wasn't some guy caught up in having to follow orders he didn't agree with. He simply didn't give a shit.

"You know," said Miller, loudly. "If you like all that gear, I've got something really good stuff you all might be interested in. But you won't find it in that SUV."

"Oh yeah?" came the sarcastic reply. "And that wouldn't have anything to do with your imminent death?"

Miller shrugged. "Hey, I'm living on the edge. I'm

going to die at some point. Might as well be now or later. Doesn't matter so much to me."

"Then why even try to stall us with the mention of some secret you've supposedly got somewhere?"

"Makes it all more fun," said Miller, flashing a big grin. "I learn something new every day. If I live another day, maybe I'll learn something new. Or more importantly, have some fun."

"What have you got?"

"Oh," said Miller. "Just one of those radios."

That got their attention.

They finally turned to look at him.

The leader, the one with the beard, walked over to Miller. He stood close to him. Miller could smell his heavy, rotten, hot breath. He felt it on his neck as the leader's eyes bored into him.

Miller kept the grin there. Might have been the hardest thing he'd ever had to do.

But he did it.

"What kind of radio?"

"Oh," said Miller, speaking slowly, to draw it out. "One of those shortwave radios. Good for communicating long distances, you know."

"A shortwave radio?"

"Yup," said Miller. "Why? I doubt you guys would be interested in something like that."

"Well," said the leader, pushing his pasty white face incredibly close to Miller's. "It wouldn't work anyway. The EMP was strong enough, at least around here, to wipe out almost all electronics."

"You'd think that, wouldn't you?" said Miller.

The guy's teeth were horrible. They were all rotten. Maybe that was where the smell was coming from.

"You've got five seconds to say what you're going to say, so spit it out."

"Five seconds before what?"

"Before I kill you."

He took a pistol from a holster at his side, and pressed the cold muzzle against Miller's temple.

But he wasn't going to shoot. His boss wanted a shortwave radio too badly.

This was good. And Miller knew it. He had some power over them. And he now knew that the rumors were true. Those two hikers hadn't been lying, and they'd had the correct information. These militia guys would do nearly anything for a radio.

"I've been preparing for something like an EMP for a long time," said Miller. "I shielded the shortwave radio with a Faraday cage. Rudimentary and homemade. But it does the trick."

Miller knew that these guys probably didn't actually know what a Faraday cage was or how it worked. But he could tell by their expressions that they'd heard the word before. They knew enough to know that they needed a radio with a "Faraday cage."

Now it was just a matter of making that information work for him. Miller hadn't quite figured that part out of it. If only he'd had more time before he'd run into these guys.

"Here's the deal," said the leader. "You're going to take us to this supposed radio of yours. If you don't, we're going to kill you. Only first, we're going to torture you. You're going to tell us where it is. Trust me."

"You know," said Miller. "I was thinking that this radio might come in handy. Pretty useful for communicating with other groups across the country. Pretty useful for consolidating power, if you catch my drift."

"You sound like you know what you're talking about, but you don't know shit."

"I know your boss really wants this radio," said Miller. "And he's going to be upset if you screw it up. That couldn't be good for you. The best thing you could do is take me directly to your boss. I'll tell him the location of the radio."

The leader laughed, throwing his head back and letting out a disgusting cackle. It really showed off his bad teeth.

"There's no chance in that. Like I said, you're going to take us to the radio right now."

"I'm only dealing with the boss," said Miller.

The punch came fast. The leader's hard fist caught Miller in the temple.

Miller reeled with the blow. He saw stars. But he took it as best he could.

"Make it easy on yourself, and you might just live."

"The boss," said Miller. "Or you're not getting it."

Another blow. This one connected with his jaw. Pain flared through his face. Miller reeled again, almost falling.

But he was a big man with a barrel chest. Well built. He didn't fall. It'd take more than a couple punches to fell him. He may have been a white-collar professional before the EMP, but that didn't mean he wasn't physically tough. As tough as they come.

"I don't know what you're thinking. I don't know what you're planning. But don't think we're dumb enough to take you to our boss without the radio. He's not going to like that. It's simply not going to happen."

"That's the only way you're getting it," said Miller.

There was blood in Miller's mouth. Maybe a tooth had gotten knocked out. He wasn't sure.

The leader reached into his pocket and pulled out an automatic knife. He hit the button, and the blade flashed out. Double-sided, like a dagger. And it looked sharp.

"We'll make you talk. And you'll die. I don't partially enjoy torturing much myself, but Kenny over here," he said, nodding his head to the guy who had the shotgun pressed into Miller. "He's a sick freak or something. He gets off on slicing people to ribbons. I've watched him do it."

Maybe they were bluffing. Maybe not.

Miller decided to wait it out for as long as he could. Take his chances. Because if this plan didn't work, he couldn't take out these four guys by himself.

He'd almost convinced himself that there really was a radio. Of course, there was nothing. He'd have to lead them to a place where he could take them out.

"You've got two seconds."

"Boss or nothing," said Miller.

"Whatever, have it your way. Here you go, Kenny." He went to hand the knife to Kenny.

The shotgun moved away from Miller's belly.

"I've got my own, boss," said Kenny. Delight dripped all over his words.

Miller watched as Kenny took something like a Bowie knife from a leather sheath.

"Remember," said Kenny, pointing the knife at Miller. "You asked for this."

Miller figured they'd just try to scare him. Maybe drag the point of the Bowie knife across his skin. Maybe draw some blood.

That was the best case scenario.

It was almost too fast when it happened. Miller felt a hand on his. He felt his fingers being tugged away.

The knife flashed as it sliced downwards.

Pain in his hand.

Miller wasn't sure what happened. The pain was diffuse. What had been hit?

Miller looked down at his hand.

His pinky was missing. Completely gone, down to the knuckle.

Blood flowed freely, already pooling on the ground.

Kenny just laughed.

The leader laughed.

The two others chuckled nervously. Maybe they were worried that a similar fate awaited them too, if they didn't stay in line.

The blood kept flowing.

No one spoke for a long moment.

Miller didn't know how long he'd last, bleeding out like that. But he didn't move to put pressure on the wound, or to raise it above his head. It needed more attention than that, anyway.

"Here's the deal. This is your last chance to come clean and cooperate with us. If not, I'll set Kenny loose on you. And I mean really loose. You wouldn't believe what he's capable of. He's a sick man."

Miller knew he was out of options.

"OK," he said. His voice sounded funny to him. Maybe it was the adrenaline coursing through him, as his body responded to the wound. He felt a little shaky. "I'll take you to the radio."

"Good."

Now all Miller had to do was figure out what the hell he was going to do.

11

MAX

The pickup truck came speeding towards them. It looked like two drivers in the cab, and no one in the back. The bed looked empty. It was an older truck.

They all had their rifles ready.

Max's hand was on his Glock.

The driver of the pickup didn't hesitate. Whoever it was drove it right up to them, stopping only about twenty feet away.

They weren't acting like they were looking for a fight.

The engine cut off.

The highway was silent once again.

"What do we do, Max?" said James. His voice sounded shaky.

"Stay calm," said Max.

Max walked, Glock ready, towards the pickup.

He could see through the windshield more clearly now. There was only one person. Someone with long hair.

A woman?

The driver's side door opened.

A woman stepped out.

She was tall, with long legs clad in tight black jeans. Her hair was thick and dark, tied behind her head in a messy ponytail.

She wore a gun on her hip, but she didn't reach for it.

Not yet, at least.

She and Max locked eyes.

"You're entering our territory," she said.

"Whose territory?"

"Ours," she said.

"You represent a group?"

She nodded.

She was in her early forties, most likely. Her face was pretty, with slightly angular features. No makeup. Her expression was serious, and she stood tall and didn't waver or quake. She seemed like someone who was sure of herself and used to getting her way.

"Look," said Max. "I don't know who you are, or what group you represent. But we're just passing through. We're not looking for any trouble."

She just stared at him.

"What's the name of your group?"

"We don't have a name. We're a self-sufficient democratically organized community."

Max nodded. "That's great, but you don't own the highway. As far as I can tell, it belonged to the people of the United States. The EMP didn't change that, even if the government has fallen all over. And it seems like it has."

"How many of you are there?"

"Six."

"Men, women, children?"

"Three women, three men. No children."

Max didn't consider James and Sadie children. They were quickly becoming adults.

"Where are you headed?"

"That's our own business."

Max didn't want to reveal their plan to head to Kentucky. He didn't know who this woman was, and while she didn't seem interested in physically harming them (she wouldn't have been a threat, anyway, against them all, or even Max alone), she could do damage to them in some other way.

"My name is Kara," said the woman, taking the conversation in a new direction. "You should come with us. We welcome newcomers to our group."

"We're not interested in joining."

"You might change your mind once you see our community. We've been building it for years before the EMP. We have medical facilities, showers, bathrooms. We grow our own food."

"Not interested."

Max didn't trust her, or her supposed community. It was better to strike out on their own, take matters into their own hands.

"You could come and see what it's like. Get a shower. Eat some food. Good food. No pressure, no obligations."

"Sounds too good to be true."

Max didn't trust her, even though she looked like a trustworthy person. Or at least as trustworthy as they came after the EMP.

"Talk it over," said Kara. "You have time."

Max didn't like to take orders from a stranger, but he was smart enough to realize that she had a point. Talking it over would be good.

Their supplies were perilously low, as they always

seemed to be. Even a single meal would do them good, allow them to continue pushing on.

And information. They could get information from Kara and her group. Information about the route ahead, about the dangers that lay in their path.

"Come on, James," said Max, walking away from Kara and heading towards the Ford Bronco.

Chad stood there, looking dazed. Max didn't know what was going on with him. He didn't bother calling him for a group discussion.

"What's going on?" said Georgia, leaning out the window of the Bronco.

Max explained the situation.

"We're going, right?" said Mandy. There was eagerness in her voice. Maybe it was the thought of a hot shower, or maybe it was just the idea of getting off the road. Hiding away, resting in some place that was safe and secure.

"Sounds like a bad idea," said Georgia.

"I don't know," said Max. "Let's at least talk it over."

Georgia had enough respect for Max that she was willing to at least consider any idea he presented. She nodded at him.

"Pluses," said Max. "Well, there's the food, the brief security, and information. I'm not saying we stay there. Just check it out and head out."

"Why don't we just move there?" said Mandy. "Sounds like what we've been looking for, right? A place to stay safe, a place to build a new life."

Max fell silent as the rest of them discussed the issue among themselves.

He knew which way the tide was turning with the group. They were tired and hungry.

He himself was badly injured. He could push himself,

but sooner or later he'd get sloppy and make a mistake. Without resting and recuperating, that is.

They couldn't go much farther with what they had.

In the end, Max simply said, "Come on, let's go. But we're not staying."

Mandy couldn't stop smiling. Even Georgia looked relived. And who could blame them? After all, it all sounded too good to be true.

And that was exactly what worried Max.

12

JOHN

The four of them had walked for days. They'd taken the back trails. Derek and Sara hadn't been lying about their experiences as hikers. They'd hiked these trails before, and knew them well.

They also knew how to improvise with shelters. They knew how to start fires, and they even knew how to accurately identify edible mushrooms without a guidebook.

John and Cynthia had been too scared to try eating mushrooms on their way to the farmhouse. John had enough sense to know that the death cap mushroom was common in Pennsylvania, and often masqueraded as an edible mushroom.

Before the EMP, there might have been a dozen cases of wild mushroom poisoning a year in the US. John was sure that after the EMP, with people desperate for food, there'd be even more. Only this time, there'd be no emergency rooms to go to. There would be no antidotes to take. People would writhe in agony until they died, with their loved ones watching them anxiously, hoping against hope that they'd get better, but knowing that they never would.

John wouldn't have had any idea where they were if Derek and Sara hadn't been able to show him on the map.

They weren't yet at the Pennsylvania border, but they were very slowly making their way west, on the trails that wound through the thick forest.

The weather was getting that fall bite to it. It wasn't yet cold during the days, but at night, it would have been cold without a fire.

They'd decided early on to take the risk of having a campfire. Maybe it wasn't a rational decision. John didn't know. They'd all rationalized it, saying that the chance of getting spotted was worth having the warmth. Not to mention warding off animals, and cooking food.

But in reality, what the fire mainly provided was a psychological advantage. There was something comforting and fortifying about looking into those glowing embers, those flickering flames, in the middle of a cold dark night in the woods, with no one around for miles. Hopefully.

Derek and Sara's enthusiasm for having firearms had soon died down. They kept them in their packs and hardly ever took them out. They'd probably been the sorts of people who'd been opposed to firearms before the EMP. And while they recognized their importance and usefulness now, they still carried with them enough of their old attitude to make them hesitant to really begin to understand and use their guns.

John and Cynthia, on the other hand, spent long hours around the campfire examining their guns. They learned how to disassemble them, how to load them, how to check the chamber to see if there was a live round. Not to mention target practice. There was plenty of that, and gradually they were getting better. Significantly better.

Not to mention more tolerant of the defending assault on their eardrums each time they squeezed the trigger.

Both John and Cynthia tried to work up Derek and Sara's enthusiasm for guns. But there wasn't any getting around the fact that they simply wouldn't do it.

And as they progressed along their journey heading west, John grew more and more concerned. Not just about the whole gun reluctance thing, but about Derek and Sara's overall attitude. That a lot of people were good and all that. He told them stories about his journey out of downtown Philadelphia, about the horrors he'd experienced, about the viciousness of once common people, but it didn't do any good.

Part of the problem was that Derek and Sara felt at home on the trail. Sure, they were well aware that the EMP had happened, and that the world had changed, possibly forever. But their vacations, before the EMP, had always involved backwoods hiking. So to them, psychologically, they were basically just on vacation. They'd always enjoyed being away from civilization. And now they were. They enjoyed sitting around the campfire, telling jokes, while John remained vigilant, his eyes always darting around, checking for shadows, listening for strangers approaching.

Early in their journey, they'd abandoned the idea of hiking by night and resting by day. It had simply been too challenging, once the flashlights' batteries had run out. And they'd run out surprisingly quickly.

When the clouds were thick in the night sky, there was hardly any light at all. Certainly not enough to walk by, even with darkness adjusted eyes.

John didn't know what was going on, but he'd noticed that his own night vision was getting worse. Not that the others could see well either. But when they could see a little at night, he could see nothing at all. Just a curtain of blackness and nothing else. Maybe it was a vitamin deficiency, or maybe his eyes were just going bad. He didn't know, and it wasn't like he could hop on over to his general practitioner for a checkup.

They were hiking along a trail that was wide enough to walk two abreast. Derek and Sara led the way, chatting as if they were on their honeymoon hike again.

John and Cynthia walked about twenty feet back.

"We've got to do something," whispered John. "They're not listening to anything we say. I don't know what's going to happen when we come across danger."

"But what can we do?" said Cynthia.

"Maybe we should break off and let them go their own way."

"They're better off with us, though."

"This isn't a charity. We've got to get something out of this deal. It's not our job to protect them. Plus, they're just as much of a danger to us as they are to themselves."

"You really think it's that bad?"

"Yeah. It's definitely that bad."

"Well, we can't leave them anyway. They're the ones who know where to go."

"Right."

John knew she was right.

The only option John could think of was to figure out the path on their own. One way to go about that was to be open with Derek and Sara and simply explain things to them. That might not go over so well. But John didn't want to have to be sneaky about it.

"Doing OK back there?" called Derek, turning over his shoulder.

He had a big smile on his face, like he was just out for another jaunt in the country with his lovely wife.

John flashed him a smile and gave him a thumbs up.

As Derek turned around, John's smile fell off his face immediately. He fell deep in thought, ruminating on the possibilities.

It was only about ten minutes later when they came across him. He was the first person they'd seen so far in their trip.

He was outfitted like a hiker, wearing a big backpack. He was wearing those zip-away pants, and a thin button-down sports shirt. He even had one of those adventuring hats.

He didn't seem to have any weapons on him, except for a fixed blade in a leather sheath on his belt. It looked like a custom, but John wasn't sure.

Derek and Sara waved the guy down, and stood there chatting happily with him while John and Cynthia hid in the background.

"You think he's a danger?" said Cynthia, in a low voice. "He looks harmless enough."

"We can't be too careful."

"He looks fine."

"Doesn't mean anything. He could be anyone. He could be capable of doing anything."

"What if he's thinking the same thing about us?"

"I hope he is. It'll make him more hesitant to try something."

From John's perspective, the scene was simply too weird. The three others were chatting like they'd just met at the summit of a particularly difficult climb. They weren't acting like the world had fallen apart.

"Hey there," said John, finally walking up and introducing himself.

"Nice to meet you. I'm Drew."

"We were just talking about how Drew should join us," piped up Sara. "He's an experienced hiker. We thought it'd be good to have another member of the party."

Drew nodded enthusiastically.

"And he knows a shortcut," said Derek. "Up ahead, he says there's a way to shave off a few miles."

"Close to five," said Drew, flashing a grin.

"I don't know," said John. "Can I talk to you for a second, Derek?"

"Uh, sure."

John took Derek off to the side, glancing out of the corner of his eye at Drew.

"Look," said John. "We've got to be careful. We don't know who this guy is."

"Come on, John. Enough of this paranoid crap. Just because the EMP happened, it doesn't mean everyone's turned into some evil enemy. I know you've been through a lot, but you've got to lighten up and recognize when people are willing to help you."

"I don't like him," said John.

"Well, Sara and I do. I'm not going to fall into your way of looking at things. You're too pessimistic."

John had things he could have said, but he didn't say anything except, "Maybe Cynthia and I should head off on our own."

Derek nodded stiffly. "If that's the way you want to do it. If you're that paranoid."

"Look," said John. "I'm sorry it's ending this way. But

it's your choice, how careful you want to be. And it's our choice, too."

Derek nodded. He didn't say anything, but he had that look to his face, like he was getting angry. Very angry.

"We've helped you out," said John. "With the guns, with gear. You could help us out by giving us the maps you have. The trail maps."

"No way."

"You already know the trails. You don't need the maps, but we do."

"That's the breaks."

The tension was thick between them. John could feel it.

"We've helped you out."

"Not really."

John knew that wasn't true.

He saw Derek's hand forming into a fist. Derek was bigger than he was, and taller, and he wasn't as worn out as John was. Derek and Sara had essentially had a leisurely walk since leaving the suburbs, and they were in shape and used to hiking. John, on the other hand, had to fight for his survival almost every inch of the way. He was tired and he knew it.

John had to make a decision. Leave, without the maps. That was one option. Take the maps—by force. That was another. It involved his gun. And he didn't want to do that. He wasn't going to hurt Derek. Or Sara. They may have made him angry, and they may have been stupidly naïve, but they weren't bad people.

The other option was to keep going with them, keep an eye on this new guy Drew, and try to come up with a plan soon in order to break away from the group with Cynthia.

"What's going on, guys?" said Cynthia, coming up to them.

"Nothing," said John.

"You guys coming then?" said Derek, looking at John expectantly.

John nodded. "Yeah, let's go. I hope this shortcut is good."

"Oh, it is," said the new guy Drew, flashing his annoyingly wide smile at them all.

The five of them started off again.

Once again, John and Cynthia hung back, away from the others.

"This is crazy," whispered Cynthia. "Don't you think so? This guy could be anyone. He could have stolen all that hiking stuff."

"I know. But we're just going to follow them long enough to figure out a plan. Figure out a way to keep going on our own. If that means stealing the maps, then that's what it's going to be."

"Seriously? You don't seem like that kind of person."

"Maybe you don't know me that well. I'm not above stealing. He won't give us the maps, or even tell us where to go. Derek wants us along for the added insurance. He knows we can shoot, and he can't. He doesn't want to get his own hands dirty."

They walked for another half hour, taking the new guy's shortcut, which was a thin trail, barely maintained. It was overgrown enough that John had to keep pushing branches aside. As he walked, his hand stayed close to his gun in its holster at his side. He wasn't going to be caught by surprise. He kept alert, his eyes constantly scanning.

13

DREW

Drew had done it. He'd snagged a live group. It was like fishing. You had to wait and wait, and for a long time it seemed like no one would come along. And when they had come along, Drew wasn't sure if they'd bite or not.

He could barely believe it when they'd taken the bait. They'd bought his whole spiel about being an experienced hiker.

It hadn't been hard for Drew to fake it all. Faking was what he was good at. He could don a persona the way an actor does when auditioning for a big role.

Before the EMP, Drew had been something of a con man. No, he'd never gone to jail. And it wasn't that he'd never gotten caught. It was just that he was clever enough to keep all his schemes above-board, legally speaking.

But that didn't mean that there weren't victims. Drew had drained more than his fair share of bank accounts, and all through legal means. In fact, before the EMP, he was just about getting ready to settle down and retire. He had enough in his offshore bank accounts, not to mention his safety deposit boxes and crypto-currency investments, that he could live comfortably abroad for the rest of his life. That was the magic of favorable exchange rates, not to mention hoodwinking people out of their life savings.

He'd been ready to live like a king. He'd been ready to live the life that he felt he deserved.

But the EMP had changed it all.

Drew wasn't dumb. He was deviously clever, able to read people and situations with ease. He knew, after the first week, that everything had come tumbling down. Much faster than expected.

And that meant that all his hard work had amounted to exactly nothing. His money wasn't even just a string of zeros in a computer bank somewhere. Those computers weren't on, and they likely wouldn't ever be again.

He had nothing.

Nothing except the skillset he'd spent his life honing.

When he'd been in the business world, he'd always looked for the meanest, most ruthless guys to team up with. Sure, they wore suits and didn't *look* vicious, but Drew knew well that appearances didn't mean anything. Drew had been able to align his own skills with that of people just as vicious as him. And that was how he'd made the real money.

So after the EMP, Drew quickly teamed up with the most vicious guys he could find. He knew that he could use their muscles and they could use his brain. He'd be the leader, and in that way he'd get what he wanted.

And he didn't want to just survive. That was just the foundation. Soon, he'd move his way up the ladder. Soon, he'd amass his own little fortune here in the post-EMP world.

First, though, he needed the basics. And they were severely lacking in that.

After making his way out of Philadelphia, he talked his way out of any problem he came to, and when he couldn't do that, he resorted to cold-blooded violence.

Drew had taken a car to an upstate penitentiary. There, he'd found the prisoners freed. The electronic security system had shut down, and the guards had all fled. The prisoners had had no option but to escape, unless they wanted to starve to death.

Drew felt sympathetic towards them. He saw himself in them. After all, if he'd been born with a little less intelligence, he would have wound up there himself.

Many of the prisoners had already left, but others hung around, not sure what to do. It'd been years, if not decades, since they'd been out in the real world. Many didn't understand the consequences of the EMP, and many were confused. They spent their time milling around the outskirts of the defunct penitentiary, unsure of what to do.

People who were unsure of what to do were the easiest to manipulate. That was what Drew had always found. And that instinct didn't fail him. Soon, he had his little band of big, muscular, vicious guys.

Unfortunately, things hadn't gone exactly as Drew had planned. A powerful militia group had formed in the suburbs, recruiting many of the prisoners, and Drew and his group found themselves unwelcome unless they submitted to the authority of the new boss.

So Drew and his group had moved north, with plans to build a community there, on the outskirts of the new "government" that was developing in the suburbs.

Pushing On

The group of his four big guys was lying in wait along the trail.

Drew was leading the men and women he'd met right to his muscle men.

The group Drew had found was armed. But only somewhat. Only two of them had guns, at least visible guns.

One of them looked like he might be a problem. He was suspicious of Drew. Drew knew how to sense that.

But that wouldn't be a problem. His guys would take care of them all.

Drew's guys, lying in wait, were getting hungry. It was only a matter of time before they got fed up with Drew. Drew knew he had to prove himself soon, or else risk losing his little group that he was going to do so much with. He was going to lead them to great heights.

Drew was smiling to himself as the five of them walked along.

Up ahead, Drew recognized a small boulder that marked the spot where his guys were lying in wait.

"We're making good progress," called out Drew.

"We're lucky we found you," said Derek.

"No," said Drew. "I'm lucky I found you."

14

MANDY

Max had been resistant to the idea, but in the end, he couldn't say no.

Mandy couldn't believe their luck. Kara had driven ahead of them, leading the way for the Honda and the Bronco, taking them all the way into the heart of the compound.

Kara, a beautiful woman who had a sort of elegance about her, gave them a tour of the community.

Mandy almost cried for joy when she saw the showers. They were rigged up so that there was even hot water. Mandy didn't listen to the explanation about how they'd gotten hot water without electricity. Probably it involved someone heating up the water over a fire. But she didn't care. It was hot water, and she was already relishing the time she'd soon spend in the shower.

It had been weeks since any of them had bathed, and while they'd all gotten used to the smell, Mandy could tell that Kara wasn't used to it. She was polite about it, but whenever she got close to Mandy, Max, Georgia, or whoever else, she couldn't help wrinkling her nose a little.

Kara and the dozens of others had been living in relative comfort since the EMP. As they toured the compound, Kara gave them a rundown of the history of the place. Basically, some friends, years ago, had gotten together and planned this thing out. Word had gotten out, and people had joined up. Most everyone who lived there now had contributed something major to the facility.

Since the community had been started before the EMP, they'd had the luxury of trips to Home Depot, of ordering supplies online, and also just simply stocking up on food and provisions.

"There's a fully functional medical facility," said Kara, gesturing off to the right. "We even have a doctor. He was a surgeon before the EMP, and he's highly qualified. Of course, he's going to have to learn to get by without x-rays and other high-tech things from our now bygone era."

Kara spoke as if the pre-EMP world would certainly never return. It shocked Mandy a little bit. Sure, that was the way Max had always talked, but secretly Mandy had held out some hope that things would eventually go back to normal. She'd hoped that the government would eventually get its shit together and basically come in and save everyone. She'd hoped that it was merely Max's own pessimism talking, but to hear it from a stranger, that was something different.

"What about the defenses?" said Max, looking around the large compound.

"Well," said Kara. "As you can see, we have concrete walls around the entire property. All our food is grown within the walls, and there's a registry for people coming and going. That way we can cut down on people sneaking in, should they find us. But as you can see, it's a pretty hard place to find. We chose it to be out of the way."

"The guards are always there?" said Max, eyeing the rudimentary towers, manned by men with rifles.

"Of course," said Kara. "We're serious here about security, if that's what you're worried about, Max."

Max didn't say anything.

"Let me show you the new crops," said Kara, pointing off to one of the fields.

"This is awesome, Mom," said Sadie, as they all moved to follow Kara.

"It's nice," said Georgia, in a noncommittal way.

"You don't like it, Georgia?" whispered Mandy, so that Kara couldn't hear her.

"It's nice," repeated Georgia. "I just want to be cautious."

"What's there to be cautious about? This is what we've been looking for."

Georgia didn't answer. Instead, she looked behind them. "Where's Chad?"

"I'll go get him," said Mandy, spotting him. "Looks like he's wandered over to that guard tower."

"Hurry back," said Georgia. She sounded nervous, as if she didn't want Mandy to get separated from the group.

Mandy didn't see the cause for concern, but she was anxious not to miss more of Kara's tour, so she hurried off towards Chad.

Mandy must have been in a good mood to go look for Chad herself, but that didn't stop her from criticizing him when she found him.

"Hey, idiot," she said, tugging on Chad's sleeve. "What the hell's gotten into you? You can't just go wandering off all the time."

"I'm fine," said Chad.

But he didn't look fine. His eyes had a dead look to them, and his pupils were small and contracted.

"Idiot," muttered Mandy, pulling him towards the group on the other side of the compound. "I know you're on something. You don't fool me."

Chad didn't say anything, but followed along dutifully.

When they arrived to where the rest of the group was, Kara was patiently explaining the different plants they were growing.

"These are potatoes," she was saying. "They're not too hard to grow, and they provide a lot of calories for the work that you put in. That's the thing we think about the most—does the reward meet the required work? That's the big question around here, and you'll hear us talking about it a lot. We have a lot of mouths to feed, and we don't want to be reliant on hunting, in case things change on the outside and it becomes too dangerous."

"Sounds like you've worked out a lot of the problems that we were facing," said Mandy.

"Well, we've had a lot of time to figure things out. And before the EMP, we had the internet at our disposal. We looked everything up."

"So you've been living here since before the EMP?"

"A few have," said Kara. "But most of us would just make occasional trips here to help set things up. It wasn't a full-time thing for us. I worked as a corporate lawyer, for instance. But I had a backup plan, and the minute the EMP hit, I hightailed it out of there."

Mandy glanced over at Max, who had a frown on his black-and-blue face.

"Cheer up, Max," whispered Mandy, nudging him in the ribs.

Max just nodded.

"I want to show you all something very special next. This took a lot of planning, but one of our guys, Jeff—you'll meet him in a moment—is a big tech guy."

Kara led them to a small shed in the center of the compound. It was rickety, but large enough for them all to get inside.

"Hey, Jeff."

A balding, middle-aged guy with a paunch sat at a small table. There was a microphone in front of him.

He nodded at Kara, and went back to doing whatever it was he was doing. Writing down numbers in a small notebook with a stub of a pencil.

"Is that a radio?" said Max.

"Yup," said Kara, smiling ear to ear proudly. "It's a shortwave radio. So we can communicate with whoever's out there. We haven't found many people yet, but they're out there."

"Didn't the EMP destroy it?"

"We had it in a Faraday cage, so it was protected," said Jeff, looking up briefly from his notebook.

Mandy now noticed that he was adjusting the radio in front of him. It had seemed too crazy, at first, to see him using a working electronic device, let alone a radio, that she hadn't even really seen it.

"That's crazy," said Mandy. "But how do you power it?"

"We have a hand-crank battery over there," said Kara, pointing to the corner. "It's rudimentary, but it works. We're hoping to hook it up to a bicycle soon."

"Pretty impressive," muttered Max, sounding reluctant in his praise. "Who have you contacted?"

"There's one other community in New York, similar to ours. We send out a daily bulletin with information, not advertising our location, of course. It's supposed to be for strangers who arrived and we take in, so that they can broadcast information about their families and things like that, about where they're headed, that they're still alive."

"Any luck so far?"

"You're one of the first groups to show up," said Kara vaguely. "Why don't we send it out now? It's about time, isn't it, Jeff?"

"Yup."

"You guys OK with that?" said Kara.

"I don't know..." said Max.

"Come on, Max, what's the harm?" said Mandy. "If there's anyone out there we know who's still alive, maybe they'll get the message at some point."

"I wouldn't mind doing it," said Georgia. "Although I'm sure my ex-husband is dead. That good-for-nothing couldn't take out the trash, let alone survive an EMP."

Kara and Mandy laughed.

"But I don't get it," said James, speaking for the first time in a while. "Nobody out there has a radio like this. Or at least not many people. So how would they get the message?"

"Basically it works like one of those old internet bulletin boards," said Kara. "We send out a message each day, and the other community, the one we have contact with, they write it all down. Then if someone comes by their community, they can check the registry. Hopefully the project will grow. Once we find others with working radios, we hope to spread the network all over the country."

"Basically it'd be like slow internet then?" said James.

"Really slow internet, yeah," said Kara, laughing.

"All right, ready, Jeff?"

Jeff nodded. "Just about."

Jeff fiddled with the dials on the radio.

"OK," he said, his voice changing to what could almost be considered an excited radio announcer's voice. It was strange to hear, coming from the man who had seemed, moments ago, to have almost no energy about him at all. "We're coming to you live from the nameless compound in an unspecified location. We've got some visitors here with us today. Let's get their names. Come on, don't be shy. Come right up to the microphone. One by one. That's it. Sorry, folks, bear with us."

He spoke as if thousands or millions were listening. But in reality, there might have been a handful of listeners huddled around the radio in the far-away New York compound.

One by one, Max, Mandy, Georgia, James, and Sadie went up and spoke their names, saying that they were still alive, which was already obvious.

"Come on, Chad," grunted Max, nudging Chad in the back.

"Oh, right," said Chad, approaching the microphone and briefly stating his name.

"Now it's getting close to dinner time, and I'd like to show you all your quarters before heading to the meal."

She led them to another series of buildings. They were made of concrete and had a cold feel to them.

"They're not pretty, but they work," said Kara. "Now, this is the building for women, and those are for the men. Feel free to drop your stuff off before we head to dinner."

"I'll keep it with me," said Max, glaring at the others in their group. He was telling them, in not so many words, to do the same.

"Whatever suits you," said Kara. "Now let's head over to the mess hall."

"Mandy," hissed Georgia, as Kara began leading the way again. Georgia took hold of Mandy's sleeve, and held her back while the rest continued.

"What? Come on, I'm starving."

"We're all hungry. Step in here for a minute. I don't want anyone to hear us."

Mandy followed Georgia back into the women's building. There were bunk beds lined up, a lot of them. The concrete construction gave the building a cold feel to it. The floor was concrete and seemed to suck the heat right from Mandy's body. And there weren't any windows. But nothing could be perfect. It was better to live, in Mandy's mind, in a concrete building than in no building at all.

"All right, what is it?"

"Didn't you notice anything strange?"

"Strange?"

Mandy's stomach had rarely felt emptier, even since the EMP. She was dying for a huge plate of hot food: potatoes, beans, and greens, by the sound of it. Although at this point, she would have eaten just about anything.

"Yeah, strange. Didn't you see the bunks in here?"

"What about them?"

"They're almost all empty. Look."

It was true. There was only one bunk that looked occupied. Probably Kara's.

"So what?"

"Walking around, didn't you notice how almost everyone here is a man? Kara might be the only woman."

"Yeah, I guess so." Mandy thought back, and realized it was true.

"Did you see the way they were looking at you?"

"No."

"Well, you should have noticed. And not just you. But me and Sadie, too. I'm worried."

"Why?"

"They're all about self-sufficiency here, and sustainability. They want their community to continue to grow. And the only way to do that? Have kids. And you know what you need to have kids?"

Mandy finally realized what Georgia was saying.

"Come on, Georgia, that's crazy. They're not like that. Let's go have dinner."

15

JOHN

John's eyes were on a branch that had snapped back into his face when it happened.

Up ahead, there was a strange noise.

Sara cried out. Derek made a noise that sounded like he was choking in surprise.

One moment, Derek, Sara, and the new guy Drew were there, in view. When John looked up, they were gone.

John stopped. His hand seized his gun and he pointed it forward. His finger was on the trigger.

He put his other hand up, letting Cynthia know to stop.

"What happened?" said Cynthia.

John didn't answer.

A scream up ahead.

John didn't know what to do. Did he turn back and flee with Cynthia? Or did he try to rescue the annoyingly naïve Derek and Sara?

Obviously, there was some kind of trap.

Probably Drew had led them into it, but John wasn't sure.

"Stay there," whispered John.

"If you're going, I'm coming."

"No way. Stay."

"You're an idiot."

That was Cynthia's way of trying to be endearing. It had come out slowly, her way of using insults to show affection and devotion. John was used to it.

The branches on the side of the trail were thick. There wasn't much hope of heading off to the side and approaching from an unexpected angle.

Plus, who knew how much time there was left.

John rushed forward, hoping that the element of surprise would be on his side.

He came into a small clearing, off to the side of the narrow trail.

Someone huge, wearing all orange, lunged at him.

The guy's weight was massive. He knocked John down.

John didn't drop the gun. He kept his grip tight.

The guy was on top of him, pushing down.

John could barely breathe.

Somewhere nearby, someone cackled. It sounded like Drew.

John could only see his attacker's huge, ugly face, full of long red scars. He was a former prisoner, judging by the uniform he still wore. His head had been shaved, but the hair was growing back slowly, patchy and sparse.

"I'll be taking this," came Drew's voice, his face unseen.

Another hand reached down to the gun.

But John wasn't going to let it go.

He tried to move his arm, angling the gun so that he could threaten Drew or the big guy on top of him.

But the big guy was pinning his arm down.

Where the hell was Cynthia?

Had she chickened out? He thought she'd been right behind.

"Shit," muttered Drew. "He's holding onto this thing good."

Drew's fingers were trying to pry the gun from John's hand.

"Just kill him," said Drew. There was a sickening delight in his voice.

So this was it.

The big guy, with one free hand, picked up a loose rock, about the side of a baseball. He raised his hand, ready to smash it into John's skull.

John writhed under the weight. He kicked his feet. But he couldn't reach anyone with them. He was stuck. Completely. He couldn't do anything.

A shot rang out.

John saw it all. Blood gushed from the big guy's temple. His expression dropped away, nothing but deadness showing on his face.

He started to fall, his weight crashing down.

Somehow, with the dead guy not actively holding John down, he was able to get out from under him. It took all his strength. He did it so quickly, so instinctively, that he wasn't even sure, afterwards, how he'd done it. But he was out.

Cynthia was standing nearby, her gun still raised, held with both hands. Determination was on her face.

John was breathing heavily as he stood straight up.

The gun was still in his hand. He raised it and pointed it squarely at Drew.

There was a scurrying in the branches on the edge of the clearing. Someone, or someones, had just fled.

"Where are the others? Derek and Sara?"

Drew just smiled. "My guys have got them."

"And they're just leaving you here?"

"They work for me. Don't worry. They'll be back."

"I wouldn't count on that."

Drew kept smiling. "Look, I'm sorry about all that with the gun. He got a little overenthusiastic. I was just trying to get the gun away from him. I don't know what he's capable of."

"You're talking about him like he's alive. Look at him."

"Yes, what a shame."

"Doesn't sound genuine."

Drew shrugged. "He was an employee. But listen, we don't need to let this little misunderstanding ruin what could be a mutually beneficial relationship between the three of us."

"You can't sweet talk your way out of this one."

"Oh, don't get me wrong. I'm not trying to do that."

"You remind me of a guy who was trying to sell me bogus siding once. And I never even had a house. Tell me where Derek and Sara are, or you're dead."

"Truth is, I don't know. I can call my guys back."

"Do it."

Drew cupped his hands to his mouth, and called out. "All right, guys, enough is enough. Bring 'em back. They're going to kill your boss if you don't."

But Drew wasn't taking it seriously. He still had a smile on his face. Clearly he didn't think that John was capable of carrying out his word.

"Looks like your guys have cut and run," said John. "They're not coming back."

"Guys!" called Drew. "You're not going to abandon your boss, are you?"

"Pathetic," muttered John.

"What are you going to do with him?" said Cynthia.

"The same that he was going to do to us."

John squeezed the trigger. The bullet struck Drew in the forehead. John's aim had gotten good. Sure, he was close to the target. But he was also a beginner.

Drew's smile fell off his face. His body crumpled to the ground. The corpse lay there, slumped, blood pouring down the front of his face. The eyes were rolled back, lifeless.

"What about Derek and Sara?"

"Shit, I don't know. Do we go after them?"

"They would have done the same for us, right?"

"I don't know about that. Remember how they wouldn't listen to us about security? About guns? And about this piece of work here?"

John pushed the toe of his boot against Drew's corpse.

John didn't want to go after Derek and Sara. It meant risking his own life at the expense of others who hadn't been willing to take care of themselves.

"Shit," said John. "We can't leave them."

"I know," said Cynthia. "We've got to go for them."

"Come on."

They made their way across the small clearing. The branches were thick at the sides. John pushed his way through. He could see a path of broken branches, where the other guys had pushed their own way through.

"We can follow their trail pretty easily," said John. "It goes without saying that we've got to be careful."

"They don't have guns, though. We've got the advantage."

"They have guns now. Remember? They'll have had time to go through Derek and Sara's packs. Guns and ammo. That's what they're going to have."

"Shit."

John shrugged. "Fortunately, I bet we're better shots than they are at this point."

"They're criminals. Don't you think they know how to use a gun?"

"Probably, yeah. But they're probably bad shots."

"That's not enough to risk our lives on."

"Yeah, but that's what the breaks are. The other option is leaving Derek and Sara to their own fate."

Cynthia seemed to consider it for a moment.

"I guess we can't," she said finally.

"Nope."

The going was hard. Even with the path having been blazed, so to speak, ahead of them, it was a real slog. The underbrush was thick and their boots sank into ground. Instead of being firm, the earth was soggy, draining their energy.

They still had their packs with them, and they were heavy. They couldn't have left them back in the clearing, for fear that someone would take them.

After half an hour, John and Cynthia were exhausted. They stopped for a moment. Both were panting with exertion, and sweating profusely. Sweating meant losing a lot of water. So far they'd tried to avoid sweating too much. But they didn't have that luxury now.

"Come on," said John. "We've got to keep going."

"Yeah, but where?"

"What do you mean?"

"There's no more trail."

John looked where Cynthia was pointing. She was right. There were no broken branches. No heavy footprints. The terrain was changing. The ground was firmer from this point forward, and the branches weren't as thick.

"Shit, what do we do now? They could have gone in almost any direction."

"I don't know."

It was hard not to feel discouraged. It was the mission they shouldn't have been on in the first place, and now it had led to a dead end. Except that it wasn't just a dead end. It was the start to a journey that might have no end. They might set off in one direction, and simply never find Derek and Sara. They might walk in exactly the opposite direction.

"This would be a hell of a lot easier with cell phones," said John.

Cynthia laughed. She seemed surprised at her laughter, and maybe a little embarrassed, as if she shouldn't have laughed, considering the direness of the circumstances.

She looked up at John.

"It's fine," said John, starting to laugh himself. "We're screwed. And if it weren't tragic, it'd be funny."

"It's a fine line, I guess."

"So where do we go?"

Cynthia shrugged.

Suddenly, off in the distance, came an ear-piercing scream.

John and Cynthia looked at each other.

John's grip tightened on his gun.

Cynthia took hers from her holster.

"Come on."

16

MILLER

They'd tied something to Miller's finger. Some kind of simple tourniquet. It seemed to have stopped the blood.

The pain was there. Weird pain. Strong and powerful, but not acute. It pulsed, coming and going in intensity.

Miller sat between the two biggest guys in the backseat of his own SUV.

They were hurtling down the road, driving fast across a mixture of paved and dirt roads. They were heading back the way that Miller had driven just hours ago.

Miller'd had no options. He'd had to tell them something. They'd wanted the location of the radio, and they would have killed him.

In many ways, Miller longed for death. It would all be over. This nightmare. If he was dead, he wouldn't be haunted by the loss of his family. Or so he hoped. He'd never been a spiritual man, and he didn't know what waited him on the other side. He'd never put much thought into it before. But now he found his thoughts drifting in that direction.

But it was better to stay alive.

He wasn't going to give up yet.

Miller was angry with himself. The anger went with the pain that radiated from his finger. He was angry that he hadn't taken the time to calm down enough to form a reasonable plan. Instead, he'd just dashed away from the farmhouse, driving at top speed. He'd thought that his plan had made sense. Enough sense, at least.

But the plan had shattered when it ran up against the reality of these hardened killers. They weren't going to fall for something so silly, so juvenile. It had sounded too easy to Miller, the whole plan, and that should have been a warning sign to himself.

Miller hadn't known where to tell them the radio was. Of course, there was no radio. So what he'd needed was a place where he had some chance of killing these guys, or at least escaping himself, as unharmed as possible.

He'd debated about whether to tell them to go to the farmhouse. On one hand, if those people were still there, Max's brother, whatever his name was, then it gave Miller a chance of surviving. But it also would put them all at risk.

In the end, Miller was so bent on revenge he told them how to get to the farmhouse.

He figured the people there would be able to take care of themselves. They had plenty of guns, after all.

But Miller was racked with guilt. Maybe he'd end up being responsible for the death of other innocents, not just his own family.

"Is this the place?"

Miller looked out the window. It was the driveway to the farmhouse all right.

"Yeah," said Miller.

The pain in his hand was bad.

"Keep driving. This is the place."

The atmosphere in the car was tense. The guys seemed more nervous than Miller. And that was strange, since Miller seemed to have more at stake.

These guys had no idea that Miller was trying to lead them into a trap. And they didn't seem concerned about the possibility. What they seemed more concerned about was getting or not getting the radio that their boss so desperately desired.

By the way they talked, it sounded as if their boss was just as vicious with his own men and women as his enemies.

"He'll reward us, though," said one. "If we get it."

"I hope. It could be good. But it could be bad, too. Really bad."

"How so?"

"What if it's the wrong radio? What if it doesn't work?"

"You mean we're going to disappoint him?"

"Yeah, and trust me when I say you don't want to see the boss disappointed."

"Oh, I know. I've already seen."

"Come on, you didn't see shit. You just joined us a week ago."

"I saw him cut the throat out of some woman."

"One of us?"

"Yeah. She'd fallen asleep instead of doing her assigned patrol."

"Well, she deserved it then."

"I mean, yeah, she deserved it. But having her throat cut out?"

"What do you mean cut out? You mean he slit her throat, right?"

"No, that would have been better. He just stabbed her, then dug around... literally digging out whatever the hell is in there. She was alive for most of it."

"Sounds like something Kenny would get up to."

"I hear that," said Kenny, chuckling.

"So you scared or what?" A bit of a mocking tone.

"Not scared. Let's just hope we get the right damn radio."

"Is this the place?"

Someone jammed the butt of a gun into Miller's ribs, stirring him.

Miller looked up. They'd driven down the driveway and now they sat in front of the farmhouse. It was battered and weather-beaten. But there it was.

The sunlight was dropping fast on the horizon, hidden behind the trees.

No lights shone in the house. Not a good sign.

Had Miller made another mistake? Maybe they'd already left.

"Come on, asshole."

Someone grabbed Miller by the collar and dragged him forcibly out of his own SUV.

"You think he's leading us into a trap?" said Kenny.

"Probably."

"What do we do then?"

"What do we do? Is this amateur hour? We send him in first, that's what."

"How's that going to help us? If he's got friends in there, it'll just help him."

"Whatever. Who do you think I am? Some kind of genius or something? We just send him in. End of discussion."

The rest of them muttered vaguely mutinous things under their breath, but Miller wasn't paying attention.

Miller wasn't going to balk at the leader's bad strategic thought. Even if everyone had already left the farmhouse, and Miller was all alone, going in first might just give him the chance he needed.

"Come on, get going."

Another jab from the butt of a gun.

"Don't want us to cut off another finger, do you?"

Miller walked slowly towards the farmhouse.

He was trying to take as much time as he could. He needed the time to think of a plan. But nothing was coming to him. Nothing at all.

Normally he was resourceful. Normally he was quick and strong.

But the strength seemed to have drained out of him. Maybe it was the disappointment of his dumb plan failing so horribly. Maybe it was the loss of his family finally hitting him with full force. Now that the anger was gone, sadness would come rushing in.

"Hurry up. We don't have all day."

"Yeah, asshole, hurry up."

Miller reached the door and turned the handle.

He went inside, leaving the door open. He didn't want to give them an excuse to think he was up to something.

"Give him a minute," Miller heard one of them say. "And then we go in."

"This plan still doesn't make any sense."

"Just shut up. Unless you think you're the boss. Do you?"

Miller was out of earshot now, leaving the bickering idiots behind him.

But they were heavily armed idiots.

As soon as Miller entered the living room, he knew that he was alone. Max's brother and the others had left.

That option was gone.

On to plan B.

There was no plan C.

He needed to defend himself. He needed a weapon. His mind started going to tall lamps and fire pokers, anything he could get his hands on. He'd go down with a fight if he had to go down.

But that was before Miller saw an unbelievable sight. Guns. Lots of guns. Still in the living room.

Miller could barely believe it.

Miller had been counting down in his head, as best he could. Counting down from 60.

He was at 30 now. That meant 30 more seconds before they came in. If they stuck to their plan, which was unlikely. Maybe they'd be in sooner, maybe later.

Miller dove down to the guns. He ignored the pain in his hand as he tried to match ammunition with firearms. Everything had been all jumbled up, as if someone who didn't know what they were doing had tried to make sense of all the guns and ammo.

Fifteen seconds left. It was getting close.

Miller heard heavy footsteps. They were coming.

It felt like an eternity was passing as Miller searched for a gun that had ammo.

Finally, he found it. An M&P compact, already loaded. Miller knew his guns. He checked it. He flicked off the safety.

He couldn't take them all. Not like this.

But he could get one. Then run. And then get the next one. And on and on until they were all gone and only Miller lived.

That was the plan, anyway.

Miller had spent plenty of time at his own target range, on his own property.

He crouched down, one knee on the ground, using a wall as partial cover.

He held the gun in front of him, finger on the trigger. His left hand, bloodied and throbbing with pain, wasn't much good to steady his right hand with. He did the best he could, gripping his left hand around his right hand's wrist.

He took a deep breath.

The footsteps were louder.

Miller didn't have much time to think. The last thing he remembered thinking was, "How could these guys be stupid enough to give me this chance?"

Maybe this chance was the only one he had. It was the only one he needed.

One of the nameless underlings entered first. Gun in hand. His expression registered shock. Only briefly.

Miller squeezed the trigger twice. Hit the guy in the chest. He went down with a thud.

Someone barked orders outside.

Miller didn't have much time. He was up in a flash, dashing out of the room, towards the back of the house.

The way he saw it, he had two options. Head out the back and try to escape into the woods.

Or stay in the house and fight.

Miller's foot hit the bottom of the staircase. His body had made the decision for him. It was better that way. Better not to let the brain get too involved. Thoughts and feelings had nothing to say now. Nothing good. Miller was running on pure instinct.

"He's heading upstairs!"

A shot rang out behind Miller. Pieces of the ancient plaster wall scattered in the air. The bullet was lodged in the wall.

Miller made it around the corner at the top of the stairs.

Another shot.

Miller got into position. As best he could, around the cover of the wall.

"Careful. He's waiting for you."

Miller controlled his breathing. He kept it low and shallow, hopefully not audible.

The footsteps on the staircase were heavy. Was it one of them or two?

Miller's trigger finger was itchy. This may not have been the revenge he'd dreamed of, but it was revenge nonetheless. It might be all that he got.

There were only a few seconds left before they got up the stairs.

For a second, Miller closed his eyes, pulling up remembered images of his wife and son. They'd been at a local summer picnic, only weeks before the EMP. They'd been eating watermelon, and laughing at how much Miller had managed to get on his button-down blue shirt that his wife had bought him for his previous birthday.

So much had changed.

If only there was a way back.

The footsteps had reached the last step. Miller knew because it squeaked like hell.

Miller's eyes were open and he was ready.

17

KARA

The group of new people was happily eating their dinner, asking for second helpings of everything. While Kara had already grown tired of the food, the newcomers were happy to gobble it up as if it was the best thing they'd ever eaten.

"Excuse me for a minute, will you?" said Kara. "I've got some business to attend to."

"This is amazing," said Mandy, smiling up at Kara.

"Glad you like it," said Kara, her professional smile on her face.

Kara saw Max glancing at her. There was suspicion in his eyes, and a dark look on his face. And that was aside from all the bruises.

Max didn't trust her. And that might turn out to be a problem.

Kara took her plates to the wash station in the mess hall, and made her way to the exit. On the way out, she passed by Jeff, who was eating at the end of a long table filled with men.

"I've got to talk to you. Meet me outside," she whispered, leaning down and speaking right into his ear.

As soon as Kara exited the mess hall, that smile she'd been flashing all day fell away. Her face was serious.

In her pre-EMP life, she'd learned how to put on what she'd always called the "client face." It was a good way to earn trust and inspire confidence. But she'd always found it exhausting, and at the end of the day, it always fell away and she was left with her normal somber face.

She knew she was a good-looking woman. To Kara, her body was just another tool at her disposal. Sure, she liked it just fine for what it was, a body. She knew that her appearance was a big reason that she came across as trustworthy. Before the EMP, she had dressed professionally for work, but in a way that didn't hide her curves.

Kara was glad that she'd been able to use her abilities bring this new group to the compound. They'd be useful. They were exactly what the group needed.

"What is it?" said Jeff, sidling up next to her.

Unless he was on the radio, he always came across as incredibly low energy. Almost like a sloth. Or worse. But if you could look beyond that slovenly body of his, and the slow-moving eyes, you'd see that in that skull of his, there was a brain that was always running at top speed. He was always calculating, always thinking, always scheming. He wasn't a bad guy. He certainly wasn't evil. And neither was Kara. But they both shared a common interest, and that was the continuation of their community. At any cost. No matter what the others thought.

"I'm worried about that one guy."

"Max?"

"Yeah, the one who always has that brooding look on his face."

"He could be trouble."

"You picked up on it too?"

"He doesn't trust us."

"And should he?"

"We've got to do what we've got to do."

"You think the others will go along with it?"

"The others in the compound?"

"Yeah."

"We'll make them think it's a democracy. Just as our constitution says."

"But you and I know how to get things done, how to arrange everything just right."

"Exactly."

"We're going to make a good team."

"We already do."

"So what's the plan?"

Kara paused for a moment, staring out into the woods. This was the perfect spot for the compound. There was nothing around for miles. It was community-owned land, an old forgotten tract of land that had once, long ago, belonged to some railroad baron. They'd all chipped in, some of them more than others, and purchased the land about ten years ago. As the numbers of the group grew, the newcomers had chipped in more money, lowering the cost for anyone.

Not that money mattered anymore. It didn't matter who had paid for what. At least not in the minds of many. Kara, on the other hand, thought differently. She'd earned an easy six figures year in and year out, and she'd paid more than most in their group. And she felt that she deserved to have more say in matters, rather than exist as a single voice in a democracy of dozens, each with an equal amount of power. That was where her scheming with Jeff came in. He thought along the same lines.

"You really think everyone will vote to keep them captive? Against their will?" Jeff's voice interrupted Kara's thoughts.

"Look, everyone's a realist. They just don't always admit it to themselves. That's where we come in. There are dozens of men. I'm the only woman. We knew it was a problem all along, but no one took it seriously."

"I think no one really thought something like the EMP would happen."

"Exactly. We all talked like we believed it. Like we really did. But people are more comfortable just going along with normal life. We can't continue this community with just men. It's not going to work with me as the only woman."

"No, it's not."

"I don't know if the older one…"

"Georgia, you mean."

"Yeah, Georgia. I don't know if she's of childbearing age."

"I don't know either. But it doesn't hurt to try."

"And other one is too young."

"But in a few years, she'd make a fine mother."

"Others might come along."

"Good, we need more. We need to start collecting women now."

"Collecting? I don't think fellow members of your gender would appreciate the way you're talking."

Kara laughed. "I've never been into all that stuff. I'm a realist."

"That's why I like you."

"I'll take care of the voting," said Kara. "I'll get the

newcomers in the showers and out of the way, and I'll hold an emergency meeting. They'll vote for forced conscription."

"You do have a way with words. But what about the troublesome one, Max?"

"He might try to interfere."

"I've got an idea."

"Tell me what's cooking in that beautiful brain of yours."

"Nothing complicated," said Jeff. "I'll take him out on the grounds to show him the surrounding area. I'll make up some excuse."

"That's good, get him away from the others."

"That's just the start."

"You're going to put him out of commission, you mean?"

"It'll be easy. A bullet in the back. Put him out of his own suspicious misery. He won't feel much."

"I'm not that concerned with his suffering."

Dinner was over, and people were starting to exit the mess hall.

The newcomers came out.

Kara put her professional smile back on.

"You all get enough?" she said, keeping her tone pleasant.

"More than enough," said Mandy, smiling happily.

Kara took an opportunity to take a glance at Mandy's body. She looked healthy, with a good body. She was just the right age to bear children. She'd do well.

"Why don't I show you all the bathing facilities again?" said Kara. "There's a little trick to get just the right amount of hot water."

"We're probably filthy, aren't we?" said Georgia's daughter.

"Don't worry about it," said Kara. "You've been through a rough time. But you can get clean here."

"I'm sure I stink like crazy," said Mandy.

"Follow me," said Kara. "We're going to have our regular nightly meeting, and you can all get cleaned up while we're busy with that. Just boring regulatory stuff. Who does the dishes and that sort of thing. You'll feel like a new person once you're clean."

Kara started to lead them away.

"Hey Max," said Jeff. "Can I talk to you a minute? I wanted to get your opinion on some traps we've set up in the forest."

"I'd rather stay with the others," said Max.

"Come on," said Mandy. With a full belly, she was jovial. "We'll be fine."

Max hesitated, but only for a moment.

"What kind of traps?" he said, joining Jeff off to the side.

So far, the plan was going perfectly. Kara wouldn't have to worry about Max's suspicions much longer.

18

MAX

Maybe Max had been overly suspicious of the whole community. He had to admit that he felt better after eating. Who knew how long it'd been since they'd had a proper meal. Sure, it wasn't a fancy meal. It was simple, but it had filled them, and Max felt a renewed sense of strength, despite his injuries.

His face hurt, but not as bad as his leg. He tried to walk without limping, as much as possible, so as not to worry the others. He knew they looked up to him, and he didn't want them to lose confidence in him, lest they lose confidence in themselves and their ability to keep going.

Maybe they could spend more than a night here. Maybe they could spend a couple weeks, recuperating. Max didn't expect it to be free, not in this new economy of pure necessity. It was an economy of survival. But Max and the others could offer their labor and skills, helping the community get up and running the way it needed to. And the community would repay them in food and shelter. Sounded fair to Max.

Later, they could move on, continuing their way to Kentucky.

Kentucky seemed so far away. And even though there were the legal papers to prove that the farmhouse existed, it was beginning to seem less and less realistic.

Supposing they got all the way there, to the farmhouse in Kentucky, years of back-breaking work awaited them. A running farm didn't suddenly get up and running overnight.

Max realized he was starting to doubt himself. He shook it off. A few weeks here. Maximum. Then they'd move on.

Max was walking behind Jeff on the way to some small game traps that Jeff had set up.

Jeff moved slowly. He was a big, lumbering sort of guy. He looked peaceful, like he'd never hurt a fly.

"How much farther?" called Max.

"About half a mile," said Jeff, turning around. "You doing all right with that leg?"

"Fine," grunted Max.

The truth was, his injury was sending shooting pains through his leg. The more he walked, the more it hurt.

He did his best to ignore it.

Max had a strong sense of ethics. These people had just fed his entire group. And more than their fair share of food, too. The least Max could do was hike a mile or two and examine some animal traps. It was his way of starting to repay his debt.

Max had never liked being in debt.

The light was starting to fall, and Max hoped they'd have enough light to see the traps clearly. He picked up his pace, closing the gap between himself and Jeff.

As he got closer to Jeff, Max found his gaze settling on an odd shape printed in Jeff's shirt.

It was a gun. Definitely a gun. It looked like it was in some kind of rigid synthetic holster. Who knew what material.

But so what? It would be stupid not to carry a gun out here.

Max had his Glock with him himself.

But even so, something about seeing the gun there sent Max's mind wandering. After all, Jeff had clearly attempted to conceal his gun. He didn't wear it openly, like Max.

Why would someone carry a concealed gun in a situation like this?

"The trap's right up here," said Jeff, stopping in a small clearing. He waited until Max had caught up with him.

It was a peaceful clearing. A little creek bubbled pleasantly nearby. The surrounding trees were shorter than in the rest of the area. Mere saplings.

There was something strange about Jeff's demeanor. Max couldn't place his finger on it but it was definitely there. He would have brushed past it normally, but his thoughts turned again to the concealed gun.

"It's a pit trap," said Jeff, pointing to the trap. "Nothing fancy. But it should work."

"So what's the problem?"

"Well, it doesn't work. It should, like I said, but it's been a week and nothing's turned up. I've got these things set up all over the place, and none of them have caught anything."

Max looked quickly at the trap, but he was sure to keep Jeff in his peripheral vision. It looked like a good trap to Max, just the kind he would have set up himself, the same kind he'd read about and studied on the internet in the days before the EMP. The trap's "mechanism," if you could even call it that, were two sticks. One small and one large. The small stick ran up from the small pit, holding the larger stick in place. Once the animal entered the trap, it would knock aside the little stick, causing the big stick to fall, closing off the pit and blocking the animal's escape.

"What are you using for bait?"

"Leftover grease from the kitchen. I thought it would work."

"Might be your problem. I don't know if squirrels and such are going to go for that. There's plenty for them to eat in the woods."

"Maybe," said Jeff, seeming to mull it over. "But I think I screwed up the pit. I don't think I dug it right. I checked the other day, and some of the food was gone, but the supporting beam didn't give way."

"Huh," said Max. "That's weird."

The trap looked fine to Max.

"Why don't you have a look at it?" said Jeff. "I'd appreciate a fresh set of eyes."

"I can see it fine from here."

"You've got to really get close to see what I'm talking about."

"You first," said Max.

"Me first? What? Are you suspicious or something?"

Max didn't say anything.

He was suspicious. He didn't like the fact that Jeff wanted him to get into a particular position. The reality was that the trap could be inspected from where they stood now, side by side.

The only advantage of getting Max out in front, as far

as Max could see, was that it was a better position to attack him from.

"Come on, Max," said Jeff. "I know we don't know each other, but I don't understand what you think is going on here. We're just regular people, trying to survive. Just like you."

"I'm not moving."

Max saw it clearly. Jeff reached up inside his shirt, his hand heading towards his concealed gun.

Max was faster. After all, his gun was at his side, easily accessible.

Max had his Glock pointing at Jeff's chest while Jeff still had his hand up his shirt.

"Pull the gun out slow, muzzle facing the ground. Try to use it against me, and I'll kill you right here and now."

Jeff did as Max said. He wasn't dumb enough to do something stupid.

"Now put the gun on the ground. Slowly. Keep it pointed away from me."

"We can work this out," said Jeff. "This is all a big misunderstanding. I just wanted you to check on the traps."

"Just put the gun down."

"No problem."

Jeff put the gun on the ground.

"Now step away from it."

Jeff took two large steps back.

"Two more steps."

"Come on, Max. This is ridiculous. I know we don't know each other. But if you knew me, you'd know I'm not that kind of person."

"Then why'd you go for your gun? Two more steps."

"I got freaked out. That's all. I saw you going for yours." Jeff took the two steps.

Max knew it was nonsense. Just nothing but lies.

"What's the angle? Why do you want to off me?"

Max kept an eye on Jeff as he bent down and recovered the gun. He checked it. It was loaded.

"You're been under a lot of stress," said Jeff. "But you've got to realize that it's made you paranoid. It's just an adaptive response. Mistrust is good in a lot of intense situations, but you're among friends now. You've got to realize that."

Max knew Jeff was going to play innocent as long as he could.

There was nothing left but violence. A last resort, but a necessary one.

Max moved forward swiftly. Jeff's gun was in Max's left hand. Max drew his left arm back, and swung it around in a large arc. The gun connected with Jeff's cheek.

Jeff reeled. He toppled over and screamed in pain.

Max was down on top of him, pushing the muzzle of his gun into Jeff's temple. Pressing hard.

"Tell me," hissed Max. "Or you're dead. I'm not wasting any more time on you."

"Don't shoot me," cried Jeff. "It's not my fault... Kara, she made me do it."

"What does she want?"

"She wants the women."

"The women?" said Max, confused for a moment.

"She wants to continue the community. The only way to do that is to have babies."

Suddenly, it clicked for Max. "So what's she going to do?"

"She's going to get everyone to vote to forcibly

conscript you all. She thought you were trouble, so she made me take care of you."

"Great job on that."

"I'm not like that, trust me. It's all Kara. I can help you escape. She wants to keep all of you, never let you go."

"We'll see about that," said Max.

"You need my help. Don't kill me. I'll help you get everyone out, if that's what you want. Or you can go now, and save yourself."

"That's not my style."

Max looked down at Jeff, who looked pathetic. Despite the chill in the air, beads of sweat were dripping off his brow. His shirt was drenched in nervous sweat.

Max knew he couldn't trust Jeff. What he was saying about the women might be true. Or it might not be. He was still trying to save his own skin.

The only thing Max knew for certain was that Jeff would try again to kill Max at the first opportunity he had.

It was either Jeff or Max.

Max knew what he had to do. But he didn't relish it.

He pulled the trigger, and Jeff moved no more.

Max stood up, his leg aching. There was fresh blood on his shirt.

The moon was out, casting its milky glow on the clearing.

A noise caused Max to look over at the animal trap. A squirrel was approaching it, pausing cautiously at intervals.

The squirrel glanced at Max before diving down into the small pit. A moment later, the small stick got dislodged, and the big stick fell down, falling with a soft thud. It covered the pit, and the squirrel completely lost its cool. Max could hear it squeaking horribly, and throwing itself, as best it could, against the piece of wood that blocked its escape.

Max moved over to the pit and lifted the large stick.

The squirrel, suddenly free, didn't even glance at Max before dashing off back into the forest.

Max didn't know how he was going to do it, but he knew what he had to do. If Jeff had been telling the truth, his friends were in serious trouble back at the compound.

Max was only one man, but he had a distinct advantage: he was supposed to be dead.

19

JOHN

John threw his pack down. Cynthia did the same.

They ran towards the sound, their guns in their hands.

John was tired. Completely exhausted. But he pushed his legs, even though they felt like lead.

He could hear Cynthia behind him, panting.

Cynthia tripped. She cried out as she fell down, heavy with a thud.

John turned back to look at her. He knew he couldn't wait. The scream he'd heard had been someone in pain. There wasn't any time to go back for Cynthia.

John kept running, leaving Cynthia behind him.

"Don't move," came a voice.

John looked to his right. It was one of the criminals, still dressed in his orange jumpsuit. Small and skinny, wiry but strong. Distorted delight on his face.

The criminal pointed a gun right at John's chest. The same gun John had given Derek.

He was about twenty feet from John.

"Drop the gun."

"What's the point?" said John. "Just get it over with."

"We want to have some fun with you two."

John spat on the ground. He was fed up. Fed up and exhausted.

John pointed his own gun. As he did, the criminal fired.

The bullet slammed into John's left arm. He felt the pain, but he still took good aim, and squeezed the trigger.

John's aim had been good, but not perfect. Still, his practice had paid off.

The criminal screamed, dropping his gun. The bullet had hit him in the shoulder.

John walked forward, getting closer, keeping his gun level and aimed at the man's chest.

"Don't do it."

"Where are the others?"

"Don't know."

"This is your last chance. Tell me."

The criminal spat on the ground. "Screw you, asshole."

John pulled the trigger. The criminal fell down. A heavy thud.

Footsteps behind him.

John turned. It was Cynthia.

"You OK?" she said.

"I'm fine."

"You've been shot," she said, looking at his arm. It was bleeding badly.

"It's fine. We've got to find the others."

Another scream, off to the right.

"Come on."

John and Cynthia dashed off in the direction of the scream.

A body lay on the ground, tangled in the underbrush. It was Derek. His chest was full of crude puncture wounds.

"He's dead," said Cynthia, reaching down and feeling for a pulse on his neck.

John nodded.

He didn't waste anymore time with Derek. This wasn't the time to mourn.

Behind a cluster of thick trees, John and Cynthia found Sara. She was lying on the ground, blood coming out of her mouth. Her face was bloodied. Her nose looked like it was broken, blood flowing freely from it.

"Sara," said John. "Can you hear me? Are they nearby?"

Sara tried to talk, but it was just a gurgle of blood. She shook her head.

"They've left?"

Sara nodded. Her eyes were filled with pain and tears.

"Derek's dead," said John. He was sorry to give her the news, but he knew that she wouldn't live much longer herself.

"Come on," said Cynthia. "We can still save her, I think."

Sara's shirt was soaked with blood around the abdomen area. Cynthia lifted the shirt to reveal a bloodied mess, a cluster of gunshot wounds.

Cynthia's face fell.

"We can't do anything for her," said John quietly.

"It's going to be OK, Sara," said Cynthia. "Don't worry. We're going to get you fixed up."

But Sara's eyes were already fading.

"Come on, help me," said Cynthia, frantic. She was pushing down on the horrible wounds on Sara's abdomen, trying to stop the bleeding. Cynthia's hands were soaked with thick red blood. She was crying.

"Come on, Cynthia," said John, gripping her around the shoulders, and trying to pull her away from Sara.

It wasn't Sara any longer. Sara had died. Her final breaths were over. She was just a corpse.

"No!" cried Cynthia. "Come on, why won't you help me?"

Cynthia was sobbing. She was worse off than when John had first met her, when her husband had been shot. But she wasn't crying for Sara. She was crying for everything that had happened to her. She was crying for her husband, for Derek, for Sara, for everyone, for everyone who lived now in this horrible world.

Finally, John got her away from the body.

"It's going to be OK," he said, knowing that it was a lie, as he helped Cynthia clean her bloodied hands.

John put his arm around Cynthia's shoulder and pulled her close to him. She cried into his chest.

John knew they couldn't wait long. They had to get a move on it. They had to get their packs and keep going. They couldn't sit there, lamenting the loss of life, while the criminals were still out there. And now they were armed, more dangerous than before, and just as vicious.

"We've got to get our packs. Come on."

John stood up, and tried to pull Cynthia to her feet, but she wouldn't budge.

"We're not going to bury them?"

"There's no time. We need our packs, or we'll end up just like them soon enough."

Cynthia hesitated.

"Come on, Cynthia, snap out of it. I need you now. You've got to get my back."

Cynthia didn't answer. She'd fallen into complete despair, staring at the ground, unmoving, like a statue.

Who knew where the criminals were. Or what they were capable of.

20

MANDY

Mandy wouldn't have said that the shower had been a disappointment. In fact, it had been great. She felt clean now for the first time in... she didn't even know how long. She was grateful.

But if she was being really honest, the hot water had only lasted about half a minute, and it wasn't exactly what she would have called hot. It was more like lukewarm water, trickling down on her, nothing more than a thin stream. Forget about water pressure, like on a normal shower head. The whole setup had reminded Mandy of water coming out of a leaking gutter after a long rain storm.

There hadn't been a bathroom. No faucets. No toilet. But at least there had been privacy. Mandy was thin, but she'd had to squeeze to get herself into the cramped, dingy, dark space that approximated a shower stall.

"What do you think they're talking about?" said Sadie. "They've been in that meeting for a long time."

Georgia, Sadie, and Mandy were alone in the women's

quarters. Sadie sat on her mother's bunk, and Mandy sat on her own.

Their meager possessions were piled up around them. It was the first time in a long while that Mandy had unloaded her pack. She gazed with some dismay at the dirty and stained clothing, at the battered things that amounted to all her worldly possessions.

The concrete building was even colder now that the sun had gone down. It seemed to suck the heat right from Mandy's body. She hadn't been able to get completely dry after the shower, and the damp chill seemed to reach her bones.

She was already hungry. The big meal had only filled her for about an hour, and now the hunger was back. Maybe it was because she hadn't eaten properly in so long, and her glycogen stores were still perilously low. Or maybe because there hadn't been any animal protein in the meal. It had tasted good, even though it was simple, but was that kind of food really enough to sustain someone day in and day out?

"What are they talking about?" said Sadie, repeating herself. "Didn't anyone hear me?"

Her voice echoed a little in the large, mostly empty room.

"Sorry, Sadie," said Georgia. "I was daydreaming, I guess."

"I think Kara said it was just a routine meeting, right?"

"But it's been a long time. Over an hour. What do they have to talk about?"

"I'm sure there's a lot to talk about," said Georgia. "They're running a community here. And that means there's more than just dealing with the practical things. They've got to figure out how to govern themselves."

"It is a little weird, though, don't you think, Georgia?" said Mandy.

Mandy didn't want to admit it to herself, but she had been feeling a little uneasy since the shower. Something wasn't right, but she didn't know what it was.

"What do you mean?"

"I thought Kara would have come to talk to us or something, I guess."

"She's probably just busy with her meeting. She seems like an important person here."

"Yeah, I guess you're right. Maybe I'm just feeling a little uneasy or something from the food."

"From the food?"

"I'm not used to eating so many potatoes."

Georgia laughed.

"I'm going to get some fresh air," said Mandy.

"I'll come with you," said Sadie.

"Georgia?"

"I'm enjoying this bed too much," said Georgia. "When was the last time we got to relax on a real bed?"

It wasn't much more than a Spartan bunk, but Mandy knew what she meant.

Sadie followed Mandy to the door.

"I hope James is behaving himself and not getting into any trouble."

"You sound like his older sister sometimes."

"They say the brains of girls mature faster than boys'."

"Wishful thinking, I'd say," muttered Georgia.

"Mom!"

"Just kidding, Sadie."

The door was metal, and of simple construction. There wasn't a normal door latch. Just the type of latch you'd see on a shed door, with a hole to put a padlock through.

Mandy pushed on the door, but it didn't open.

"It's stuck or something."

Mandy pushed again. The door felt like it was hitting something on the other side of it, as if someone had put something in front of it.

"Give it a good push."

"I am."

Mandy pushed again.

"I think it's locked. Do you hear that rattling?"

"Locked? From the outside? That doesn't make sense."

"I remember there was a latch on the outside too. Maybe someone put a padlock through it."

"What's going on? Is the door stuck?" Georgia got out of bed and came over.

"I think it's locked."

"Locked? That doesn't make sense. Let me try."

Georgia pushed on the door.

"Shit," she muttered.

She pushed harder.

"Here, give me a hand."

Georgia and Mandy pushed on the door together, using all their strength, leaning all their weight on it. Sadie tried to help, but there wasn't really enough space for her to get in there and push as well.

Georgia got down on her knees and tried to peer between the very small crack between the door and the frame.

"I can't see anything."

"They locked it," said Mandy. "This isn't good."

"Let's not jump to conclusions," said Georgia.

"We're locked in?" said Sadie. "What's going on?"

"Calm down, Sadie," said Georgia. "Don't worry. It's probably a mistake or something."

"Damnit," said Mandy. "I knew I had a bad feeling in my gut, but I ignored it. I was feeling uneasy for a reason."

"You're not helping," said Georgia, glancing over at Sadie, who was starting to breathe quickly, as if she might have an anxiety attack.

"There aren't any windows," said Mandy. "How are we going to get out? Can we shoot the lock?"

"Let's not go crazy. I'll call for help. Hopefully it's a mistake. But it could be what I feared. I knew something wasn't right."

Georgia put her mouth near the crack in the door and yelled for help. "Help!" she cried out, loudly. "We're locked in here. Someone get us out of there."

Nothing happened. There wasn't any sound outside. No footsteps. No voices.

"That's it," said Mandy. "I'm going to shoot this damn lock if it's the last thing I do. I'm not going to be trapped in here like some animal."

Mandy went over to her bed, where her pack was. She grabbed her handgun, and checked it.

"There's no ammo," she said, examining the gun.

"What?"

Mandy threw the gun down on the bed. She grabbed her rifle next. She checked it, and there was no ammo either.

She started rooting through her pack furiously, looking for ammunition. But it was all gone. And she'd had plenty of it.

Georgia rushed over and grabbed her own rifle. "Nothing," she said.

"How could this have happened?"

There was nothing in any of the packs. Not a shred of ammunition.

"Those bastards tricked us. They knew we wouldn't give up our guns. So they somehow took all our ammo."

"Must have been when we were eating," muttered Georgia. She was shaking with anger.

Mandy, on the other hand, felt suddenly defeated, drained completely of energy. She let herself fall onto the bed.

"Do you hear that?" said Sadie. "It sounds like the meeting let out."

Sure enough, there was the dim sound of many voices outside, off in the distance. And the sound of footsteps.

"You girls all right in there?" came a voice from the door. It was unmistakably Kara's voice.

Mandy got up, and all three women rushed to the door.

"We're stuck in here," said Mandy.

"You assholes stole our ammunition," said Georgia.

"Let us out," said Sadie. "I have to go to the bathroom."

"I'm sorry for this," said Kara, her voice sweet and syrupy. "But it's for your own good."

"What the hell's going on?" said Mandy.

Hearing Kara's voice, now obviously fake and put on, angered Mandy. She felt an intense heat in her chest, and her hands were shaking.

"I'll tell you all about it soon," said Kara. "In the morning we can discuss the new plans."

"You're not going to get away with this," said Georgia. "You can't take our ammo like that."

"It's our property," said Kara, her voice sounding suddenly more serious. "We can do what we want. We're a self-governing community, and the community has spoken."

"And what has this so-called community of yours decided?"

"You're staying."

"What do you mean we're staying?"

"You heard me."

"What does that mean?"

No answer.

"Hello? You still there, Kara, you bitch?" hissed Mandy.

No answer. She was gone.

"Shit," muttered Mandy, sinking down onto the floor, her back slumped against the cold concrete wall.

"What did she mean we're staying?" said Sadie.

"It means we're screwed."

"What do they want with us?"

"I can take one guess. You were right, Georgia. It's too many men. They need more women."

"They fooled me with the food and the showers," said Georgia.

"What's going on?" said Sadie, sounding terrified.

"It's going to be OK, Sadie," said Georgia.

"Not if we can't get out of here, it's not," muttered Mandy.

21

MILLER

There wasn't much light, but Miller could see well enough. Well enough for what he needed to do.

The guy appeared on the top of the stairs. Miller saw the guy before he was seen himself. The guy had gone the wrong way, thinking Miller was in the other direction.

Miller opened fire. The guy fell, his body slumping down. But he didn't fall down the stairs.

Milled moved quickly. He knew he'd be in the line of fire. But if he could pull it off, it'd be well worth the risk. He exposed himself, moving out in the open at the top of the staircase. He shoved his weight against the dead guy, sending the corpse crashing down the stairs.

Muzzle flash. Another shot rang out. It missed Miller. Maybe the bullet hit the corpse. No way to know.

Another shot. The noise was deafening. Pieces of the plaster wall broke into chips, flying through the air.

The guys running up the stairs yelled as the corpse crashed into them. Miller didn't have time to look to see if they'd get knocked down the stairs or what.

Miller was out of the way now. His little trick would only buy him a few seconds.

He sprinted into a bedroom, the farthest one down the long hallway. He slammed the door closed behind him. He fumbled for the lock, and finally got it, setting that little mechanism to the vertical position.

But the lock wouldn't be enough.

It was harder to see in this room than in the hallway. But by feeling around, and seeing the dim outlines of things, Miller identified a large dresser. He pushed all his weight against it, sliding it across the floor until it blocked the doorway.

He wasn't running. He wasn't trying to merely hide. He just knew that he'd do better if he wasn't in a direct confrontation against them all at once. The best thing to do was pick them off one by one. Creating obstacles for them was the best way to facilitate those advantageous scenarios.

Heavy footsteps on the floorboards. The guys were already upstairs, checking the rooms.

"He's in this one."

There was a kick against the door.

"You can't hide forever, asshole."

Miller said nothing.

Suddenly, Miller had an idea.

He glanced at the window, and then at a small nightstand next to the bed. He knew right away it would work.

Another kick against the door.

Miller stood out of the way, in case they shot through the door, and fired two shots in quick succession through the wood.

No screams. He hadn't hit anyone. But he hadn't thought that he would. He was just trying to keep them scared, keep them from getting too complacent and being able to break through his barricade easily.

They fired four shots back. A fifth. Then a sixth. But they weren't overly stupid. They knew not to waste their ammo.

Miller seized his opportunity. While they were still figuring out what to do, Miller ran to the window and opened it. It was difficult to open, one of those old wooden frames that decides to swell at inexplicably inconvenient times. And it was hard with his missing finger. But he got it, pulling up with all his strength.

Miller had to put his handgun down on the bed to pick up the nightstand.

His plan was to throw the nightstand out the window. They'd hear the noise, and think that Miller had jumped out the window in an attempt to escape. They'd either send one guy outside or they'd both go. Miller would shoot them from the window above. And then deal with the one that remained inside, if there still was one.

He thought it was a good plan.

His finger was throbbing as he pushed the nightstand out the window.

Just as he got it out, another two shots blasted through the wooden door. One bullet embedded itself in the wall right next to Miller. The other hit him in the back, off to the side. The pain seared through him.

It happened so fast that Miller wasn't sure whether the nightstand hit the ground outside before or after he'd been shot.

His vision became even more of a tunnel as the adrenaline coursed through him.

Miller gritted his teeth, trying not to make any noise, as he fumbled for the gun on the bed.

"Did he jump?"

If Miller could just keep silent, they wouldn't know he was still in there.

But as he reached out, extending his arm, trying to get the pistol, he groaned in pain. It was simply too much, and he couldn't keep silent forever.

"He's still in there."

They started kicking the door. And slamming their bodies into it.

Miller didn't have much time left. His plan had failed, and he was badly injured. He didn't know how bad the bullet wound was, but he knew from the pain that soon he'd be too incapacitated to fight.

Miller looked around the room, a quick, sweeping glance. He needed somewhere to hide, or something to get behind. But there wasn't much there. No closet. Just the bed, and the dresser that was now jammed against the door.

The only strategic advantage he had, aside from being a good shot, was being in the room before them. They were the ones who had to enter.

Standard practice for Miller would be to stand to the side, back against the wall next to the door. But they'd be expecting him. They'd know he'd be there. It was too obvious.

Miller's heart was pounding like it never had before. He had mere seconds before they came in.

The dresser against the door was inching its way back, tap dancing across the hardwood floor, as the militia guys slammed their bodies into the door.

Miller's sweat was ice cold. He felt it on his skin. The pain in his back roared, so intense it completely eclipsed the pain from his missing finger.

This was his one chance.
His last chance.

22

JOHN

Cynthia was feeling better. She was finally not just paralyzed by fear and misery.

"We've got to do something about your wound," said Cynthia.

"We need to get the packs first. We're not going to last long without them."

"They also have the medical supplies."

"Let me just look at it. We might need to stop the bleeding now."

Truth be told, John was feeling a little weak. He could feel the blood flowing out of his arm. His heart was beating in a strange way. He could feel his blood pulsing. His feet, nose, and hands felt freezing cold, as if they'd been dipped in ice water.

Cynthia cut aside the sleeve of John's shirt.

"It's not lodged in there or anything. It grazed your arm."

John nodded without looking at the wound. He didn't want to see it.

"You're really lucky. Took away a good bit of flesh,

though. And it's bleeding a lot. I'll tie this around it."

"A tourniquet?"

"I don't think that'd be good for this situation. Let's just tie it around the wound, to create some pressure."

John nodded. He was gritting his teeth against the pain.

Cynthia twisted the shirt around the wound. She took a small stick from the ground and used it to tighten the cloth. She twisted it all around on itself, locking it in place.

"That should hold for a while."

"Good enough," said John. "Let's get those packs."

"Can you walk?"

"Of course I can walk."

John had been sitting down while she'd worked on his arm. He stood up quickly, and he felt dizzy as he did so. His vision seemed to swim before him.

"You don't look good. Are you dizzy?"

"I'm fine. Come on."

They set off. Cynthia led the way, since John was a little disoriented. He didn't know why he was feeling that way, since it didn't seem like he could have lost enough blood to cause those symptoms. But then again, maybe he had. He'd kept moving after receiving the wound, and who knew how much he'd bled without realizing it in that time.

The going was rough for John. His legs felt like lead, but he kept going.

"I think it's this way," said Cynthia, turning back to address John.

As John looked to where she was pointing, he tripped over a thick root in the path, lost his balance, and went tumbling down.

He hit the ground heavily, and Cynthia rushed over to him.

"I'm fine," he said.

"Maybe I should go get the packs myself. We can make camp here."

John shook his head. "Those others might be around. They'll find us if we stay here."

"They're probably long gone. They just want to get out of here with the loot."

"Maybe they want more," said John. "We've got to keep moving. Help me make a crutch and I'll be fine."

John handed Cynthia one of the pocket knives that he'd taken from the gear at the farmhouse. Cynthia took it, and had to study it to figure out how to open it. She wasn't used to modern folding knives.

"Like this," said John, taking it back from her, and opening it for her. "I'll do it. There's a branch over there that could work."

"You're crazy," said Cynthia. "Do me a favor and try not to exhaust yourself to the point where you're no longer any use to yourself or to me."

John got the point, and let her take the knife.

"Cut diagonally. Rock the blade back and forth to get it deep. One single cut," said John, instructing her based on something he had seen once, long ago, on the Discovery Channel. "Then you should be able to bend the branch and it'll snap cleanly off."

Cynthia did it and it worked. "Not bad," she said.

John stood up with Cynthia's help. She handed him the stick and he tested out different positions to hold it in.

"It's not like my leg's injured. Maybe I'll just use it as a walking stick. I just need a little more support."

"It'll help keep you from getting so fatigued," said Cynthia. "Let's keep an even pace. Slow and even."

"But we've got to get those packs. As quick as possible."

"I get that. But listen to me. We're not going to get anywhere if you fall down again, or get too tired. You've been shot, and you've got to take that into account. Pushing yourself is good, I get that. But sometimes, you've got to work with what you have. And what you have now is a gunshot wound and a weakened body."

"You're right," said John. "Sorry. I could get us both killed like this with my stubbornness."

"Have you always been like this?"

"Sort of. I think I'm getting a bit of a hard head from all of this."

"We're adapting," said Cynthia. "These experiences are changing us in indefinable ways. Our brains and our bodies are adapting as best they can to the new circumstances."

They began walking again, and they went slower this time. John made it.

The packs were where they'd left them, no worse for wear, except for some extra dirt on the outside.

Cynthia dug into her pack and drew out a full water bottle, handing it to John. He drank it down with delight. Plain old water had never tasted so good. Cynthia handed him some packets of dried fruit, telling him that he'd feel better once he got his blood sugar up.

"I don't know what I'd do without you."

"Same goes for you."

"Well, let's keep it that way. We've got to keep our eyes open and our guns ready. Those others could be out here."

"Not to mention anyone else that's here," said Cynthia.

"Too true."

"You're going to have to rest," said Cynthia, who was busy breaking out the emergency kit. She was examining the different ointments and bandages and trying to figure out what was appropriate for a chunk of flesh that had been ripped away by a bullet.

John shook his head. "You're right about taking our time," he said. "But we've got to get out of this area."

"It's almost night."

"Even more reason to get a move on it."

"You really think they'll be able to find us in the dark, if we don't make a fire? We can get in the sleeping bags and cover ourselves with leaves. We'll be practically impossible to see. Plus, we have no more batteries and it's going to be hard to move effectively at night."

John thought about it for a moment. "Once again, you're the voice of reason. You're right, we'll stay here tonight."

"Damn right we'll stay here tonight. You're crazy if you think you're going to make it far with that pack, not able to see a couple feet in front of you."

She was leaning down over John's injury again.

"Has it stopped bleeding?"

"Let me take the cloth off of it."

John felt the tension releasing around the wound as Cynthia got the stick out of there. She unwrapped the piece of shirt slowly.

"Shit," she muttered. "It's still bleeding."

John glanced down. It was bleeding all right. The sight wasn't exactly stomach-churning, but it wasn't pleasant either.

The blood flowed freely now, without the bandage stopping it at all.

"It should have coagulated by now."

"There's too much missing. Too much surface area, compared to a cut into the flesh, where the two sides can sandwich together."

Cynthia looked nervous. She was tossing aside items from the medical kit, muttering to herself.

"Nothing in there?"

"No, and we've got to get this to stop bleeding. How are you feeling?"

"Uh, tired. And a little..."

"Woozy?"

"Definitely."

"You're losing too much blood."

"I think so..."

John was feeling strange. Pretty odd. He couldn't put his finger on it, but things were starting to flip past him. He still knew where he was, and who he was. And he didn't think he was in any danger of dying soon.

That was what he thought, at least. But Cynthia's increasingly concerned attitude was starting to make him think differently. She wouldn't, of course, come out and say that she thought he'd die soon. But it was all in the way she moved, and the way she was rummaging through the packs, looking for something to stop the bleeding.

She pulled out a little laminated book, an emergency guide to dealing with injuries. "I'd forgotten that Derek lent me this."

She started flipping through the pages.

"We may have to do a tourniquet. But that's a short-term solution. And it can result in the loss of limb. I don't think I can amputate your arm..."

"Amputate the arm?" said John vaguely. He was feeling stranger by the minute.

The pain seemed to have gone away. Or at least he wasn't registering it anymore. He didn't know how much time had passed, and he wasn't sure where the sun was. It wasn't as bright as it had been before, but it wasn't night yet... His mind was full of vague impressions...

"OK, here's something," said Cynthia. It sounded like she was trying to keep her panic in check. She was trying to keep her voice calm. "It says sugar can stop bleeding. Do we have any sugar?"

"Sugar?"

"Yeah. John, come on, stay with me. Do we have any sugar?"

"The regular white kind?"

"Yeah."

"I don't know..."

John didn't think they'd brought any sugar... He didn't remember anything like that. But it didn't seem to matter. After all, sugar wasn't going to stop the bleeding. That was crazy. Maybe it would be better if he just laid down and went to sleep for a while. Maybe that would fix everything.

John felt his eyes closing as he lowered his body to the ground.

"John! What the hell are you doing? Keep your eyes open."

John opened his eyes. Cynthia was in front of him, rooting through the packs again. "I was carrying some of Sara's stuff, since she was getting tired easily. Here it is, maybe she had sugar in this bag..."

Later on, John remembered vaguely thinking that there wasn't any point in looking for sugar, and that there was no way a formerly health-conscious person like Sara would use sugar for anything, even though the four of them had enjoyed some organic instant coffee that Derek and Sara had been fond of from their trail days.

"Look! Sugar! I can't believe it. Maybe Derek used it. Who cares?"

Cynthia took the book in her hands again, to reread the instructions.

"I don't think eating it..." said John. "...Going to do any good."

"You're not going to eat it, idiot. Now shut up and let me concentrate."

Her fear of losing him was turning into mild hostility. John was OK with that.

"OK," said Cynthia, trying to get the idea straight in her head. "I'm going to pour this on your wound, and it's going to form a syrupy mixture and help the blood coagulate."

John was feeling detached from the whole thing. Probably not a good sign. He watched with mild interest as Cynthia poured the sugar carefully onto his wound.

"I don't know if it's getting on there," she said. She used her fingers to try to push the sugar into the wound.

It stung, but John had lost too much blood to care.

"It says you need a lot of sugar on there," said Cynthia, examining the wound before carefully adding more sugar. "Let's hope this works."

Suddenly, John realized how serious the situation was. The loss of blood had been affecting his rational thought process. But he knew now that he was close to death. If the sugar didn't stop the bleeding, it might be the end for him.

23

JAMES

James and Chad were alone in one of the men's quarters. James felt pretty good. He was full for the first time in a long, long time. He'd eaten and eaten and eaten, countless portions. They'd told him he could have as much as he wanted, and he couldn't remember the last time that had happened. Max had been brutal with the rationing, allowing them all only certain quantities of food and water.

James was relaxing on his bunk. His gear was partially unpacked from his pack, spread out around him. He was wearing a change of clothes. They were the clothes that he'd kept clean in the bottom of his pack, never putting them on. It was something psychological, in some weird way comforting to know that he had a change of clean clothes.

And now he got to wear them.

There was a weird little rattling noise from Chad's bunk.

"What're you doing, Chad?" said James, looking over.

"Nothing," said Chad vaguely.

"What's the orange bottle?"

James had only seen a flash of it. Chad had put it away quickly when James had looked over.

"What bottle?"

James knew that he was just a kid in comparison to Chad. But Chad had been acting really weird ever since Albion. James felt that he had some sort of responsibility to take care of Chad, especially since none of the other adults were around.

Where was Max? He'd been gone for a long time. The thought occurred to James suddenly.

Maybe Mandy was right. Maybe Chad was taking something. James was well aware of Chad's addict past.

James got up and moved swiftly over to Chad. Chad was concealing something in his right hand. His large fingers were hiding whatever it was. Probably the pill bottle.

"Hey!" said Chad, trying to pull his arm away from James.

But James was too fast and strong for him. He seized Chad's hand and pried his fingers open.

"Give me that!"

James dodged Chad's slow moving hands, got out of his reach, and moved out to the middle of the room.

"Vicodin," muttered James. "Isn't this the stuff you were taking before? This is why you've been out of it, putting us all in danger."

"Whatever," said Chad. "You don't know how hard I've got it."

"I know you're full of shit, that's what," said James. He was angry. Chad's decision could very well have put his own family's life at risk.

"You're just a kid. You don't know shit. Now shut up and let me enjoy this."

"You're an asshole, Chad."

"That's what they've been telling me all my life. It hasn't stopped me yet."

"Just wait until Max hears about this."

"Screw Max."

"How can you say that? He's done so much for us. Mandy told me how he risked his own life to save you from that mob."

"I would have been fine. Max thinks he knows everything. We would have been better off if we'd just stayed at the farmhouse."

"We'd be dead if we stayed there. You know that."

"Pffft. It'd be fine. Max thinks everything is like a life or death situation. But it's not that... You've all got to take a lesson from me and try to relax more. There's no point in worrying about what you can't change."

There was a loud knock at the door.

Maybe that was Max now.

"Max?" called James.

"Shit," muttered Chad. For all his big talk, James knew that Chad was still worried about Max finding out about his little secret.

The door swung open. And with some force.

A man appeared. It wasn't Max.

It was a tall stranger. He had a big build and towered over James, who was standing there with the bottle of Vicodin.

"What's that?" said the man. His voice was stern and deep.

"Uh..."

"Hand it over."

James did.

"Vicodin," said the man, examining it. "I don't know what you're doing with this, but drug use is not permitted here."

"I was just trying to..."

"I don't want to hear explanations. This is going to the pharmacy stash."

The man pocketed the pill bottle. James had a funny feeling about the way the man did it. He had a feeling that maybe the pills weren't going to a medical stash after all.

"Sorry," said James. "I didn't get your name."

The man just stared at him, still not introducing himself.

"Here's the deal. You're all going to join up with us."

"What?" said James. "Did you talk to Max already? He only wanted to stay for a little while to see how we liked it."

"Don't worry about Max."

"What? What happened?"

The man ignored James's question.

"As you may have noticed, we're mostly men here. And we need more women if we want to grow and continue."

"More women?"

"No one told you about the birds and the bees yet?"

James blushed. He was plenty old enough to understand.

"So obviously we're more interested in your female companions, but we'll let the two of you stay here too. We need men too. There's plenty of hard physical work to be done. So you can stay if you're willing to do it. And you're newcomers, so you'll be working twice as hard as those of us who set this place up. You've got to repay your debt somehow."

James didn't like the way this was sounding. Where was Max? Had something happened to him? Had they done something to him? And what was he saying about the women? They weren't merely James's "female companions." They were his mother and sister, and he was quite fond of Mandy too.

James felt anger rising in his chest as the tall man stared him down with a stern gaze, just daring him to say something.

Chad, who hadn't said anything, suddenly stirred from his bed. He stood up, and walked towards the man silently.

James stepped back to make way for Chad.

Chad had lost some weight since the EMP, but he was still a big guy. Sure, a lot of it was fat. But there was some muscle there too.

"You're trying to kidnap Georgia, Mandy, and Sadie? What the hell's wrong with you?"

James was surprised. He would have thought that Chad was too out of it to speak up.

Chad had slurred his words badly, but the meaning was still clear.

"It's none of your business," said the man. "You can make it easy or you can make it hard. It's up to you."

"I'm going to make it hard."

Chad rushed the guy, not even bothering to swing his fists. He simply jammed his body forward, trying to body slam him.

But the big guy was agile, and he wasn't screwed up on drugs like Chad. He had the reflexes Chad didn't have, and he stepped to the side.

Chad's head collided with the concrete wall and he fell down.

The guy was on top of him in an instant, straddling his chest. He pressed his thick forearm down into Chad's neck, making it hard for him to breathe.

Chad moved his mouth, trying to talk, but no words came out.

"You don't get a say in this," growled the man, pushing his arm harder down. "Don't you get that?"

Chad puckered his lips and spit in the guy's face.

James was paralyzed with fear. He was just standing there. But anger got to him. It overtook the fear, and he sprang into action.

James's bed was all the way over on the other side of the room. His rifle lay there. It was too far. The guy looked like he might kill Chad at any moment.

Chad's face was turning a funny color. The life seemed to be draining out of him. He was kicking his legs.

James had to move fast. And he had to make the right move. The man was much bigger and stronger than James. James couldn't afford to attack him and then receive a counterattack. He simply wouldn't make it.

James reached under his shirt. His fist grabbed the metal handle of a skeleton knife Max had given him. "This might come in handy sometime," Max had said, as he'd shown James how to wear it around his neck under his shirt.

The sheath was form-fitting plastic. The knife was securely inside it.

James tugged on it and the knife came out.

The big guy saw the flash of metal out of the corner of his eye.

But before he could turn, James was on him, going right for the guy's neck.

James had to get it done in one shot. Stabbing him in the back was risky.

James had the edge of the knife almost against the man's throat, his own arms wrapped around the guy. James's body was pressed against the man's back.

Chad was making gurgling noises. The weight of both James and the big guy was pressing down on him.

The guy's hands were on James's wrists, trying to keep the knife from his throat.

James pulled back with all his strength. But the guy was strong. He couldn't get the knife there.

Not yet.

James leaned back with all his weight. It was too much for the strong guy.

James felt it as the knife cut into the skin.

Max had shown James how to sharpen it. He'd given him a little lesson, saying that it was a hard skill that needed plenty of time to master. Georgia, too, had given James some tips here and there. She'd shown him long ago when he was a kid, but he hadn't retained it. The blade was still razor sharp with the fine shallow edge Max had put on it, running it along his leather belt for a final stropping.

The knife cut easily.

James pulled to the right. The blade moved across the man's throat, slicing it right open.

The man screamed. A gurgling scream. Horrible and bone-chilling.

James felt the hot blood pouring over his hands.

James pushed the guy off of Chad. He fell with a heavy thud onto the concrete floor.

James only gave the body a quick glance. He'd killed before. This was nothing new, unfortunately.

"You OK, Chad?" said James.

Chad may have screwed everything up with his drugs. But he'd also tried to defend James's family. Not to mention Mandy. That was worth something, wasn't it?

Chad nodded, sitting up slowly.

"Come on, we've got to go. We don't have much time. They'll be coming for us. We've got to get to the women."

James ran over to his pack and started shoving everything he could into it, as fast as he could. It'd been drilled into his head over and over again that the gear and supplies would often be the line between life and death. He needed that stuff. He couldn't afford to run off without it.

James had his pack stuffed in mere moments. He grabbed his rifle. It felt reassuring in his hands. But he had a funny feeling. Something was off. He checked it, and cursed as he saw there was no ammo.

Then it hit him. There'd been no spare ammo in his pack either.

Someone had taken the ammo.

"Chad! Come on!" hissed James, as he rushed over to the dead guy.

People would be coming. And coming soon.

Chad finally got up. He moved slowly. But he didn't move towards his own pack, which he hadn't unpacked or even opened.

Chad got to the dead guy at the same time as James.

"Chad! Move out of the way. I need the guy's gun. He's got a pistol on his hip."

"Get away!" cried Chad, blocking James's access with his large body.

"What the hell are you doing?"

"Getting what I need."

"You're getting those pills he took from you? You're sick."

James tried again to rush past Chad, to get the gun.

Chad turned, and with a nasty expression painted on his face, he gave James a furious shove that sent him tumbling down. James fell flat on his back, his head banging against the concrete. The fall took the wind out of him. He saw stars in his field of vision.

James's vision was blurry, but he could see clearly enough to watch as Chad's hand came out of the man's pocket with the orange prescription bottle. He had a greedy expression on his face as he took off the cap with fumbling fingers.

A noise outside. Heavy footsteps.

"McGovern? What's going on in there?" Another deep male voice.

Before James could move, someone was in the doorway, standing tall in the concrete door frame.

His face grew dark as he glanced to the ground, seeing McGovern's body with his throat slit, a pool of blood gathering around him on the concrete floor.

The man's hand flashed to his gun's holster. He drew it and raised it, pointing it to Chad.

"What have you done, idiot?" he bellowed.

Chad said nothing. Instead, he glanced at James. His eyes seemed to say something. Maybe it was an apology, like he realized he'd screwed everything up. It was hard to say, though. It was just a glance.

Chad rushed the guy, letting out a yell as he did so.

The gun went off. The noise was deafening, echoes off the walls. The whole place was a perfect echo chamber.

Chad fell to the ground, his heavy body making a thud.

James stared up at the tall guy. Fear coursed through him. His blood ran cold. He was unarmed. The only loaded gun was on the dead man, about five feet away from where James lay on his back.

24

JOHN

"How are you feeling?"

"Better."

John rose from where he'd been lying down. He moved slowly. His arm hurt.

"Let me check it."

"How's it look?"

"The bleeding's stopped."

John nodded.

"I didn't want to tell you, but you were getting pretty close there..."

"I know. I could hear it in your voice. You did a good job, though. I never would have thought of using sugar."

"Well, me neither. It was just thanks to that little book. You sure you're feeling OK?"

"About as well as could be expected. I'm still weak."

"Here, have some more of these."

"Ugh. I don't think I can eat another energy bar."

"Your body needs fuel. You lost a lot of blood."

"I can see that."

They'd made it through the night. Cynthia had kept

watch, and she looked dead tired now, with bleary, bloodshot eyes as she crouched near John. The sun was rising in the sky, casting light onto the ground. For the first time, John could see the dark splotches his blood had made on the ground. It was incredible he'd lost that much blood and still lived.

John took the energy bar from Cynthia. He struggled for a moment with the foil packaging.

"Here, give to me."

"It's pathetic. I can't even open it."

It felt like he had no strength in his hands.

"Here, let me do it."

Cynthia took the packet from him and opened it easily.

"Thanks."

Cynthia nodded.

John ate the bar slowly. It didn't taste good. He'd eaten too many of them. But even so, he began to feel a little better.

"We've got to get going," said John. "Who knows where those criminals are now."

"You're not going anywhere."

"What are you talking about? I'm fine."

"You can't even open a foil packet."

John tried to stand up, to demonstrate his strength. But as he rose, the world seemed to swim before him. He felt incredibly weak, like he might topple over.

Cynthia was at his side in an instant, supporting him, keeping him from falling.

"Easy does it," she said, as she helped him back to the ground.

"Pathetic," muttered John.

"It's fine," said Cynthia. "We'll stay here until you've gotten your strength back."

"Shouldn't take more than a day."

"We'll stay here as long as we need to."

They fell silent for a moment, as they each considered what would happen if those criminals came back for them.

"Maybe they're long gone," said Cynthia, as if they'd been discussing it rather than thinking silently themselves.

"Who knows."

"If I was one of them, I'd take that gear and get the hell out of here."

"They don't know how to use half that stuff. Remember how long it took us to figure everything out? And Derek and Sara showed us how to use a lot of the gear. Like that weird little water filter."

"I don't know where we'd be without that thing."

He was referring to a small water filter that Derek had shown them on one of the first days they were walking. It was a small, compact device that could be used as a straw, to sip from a body of water directly. Or it could be used as a filter on top of a normal water bottle, as you tilted the bottle to drink from it.

"So what does that mean?"

"That'll they'll probably come back."

"What do they have to gain from confronting us?"

"Maybe nothing. But they might think there's some reason. Don't underestimate stupidity."

"It's crazy about Derek and Sara... Isn't it?"

"Yeah, but..."

"But what?"

"I wish they'd listened to us."

"You're going to blame them? They're dead."

"I'm not blaming them. I just... it's hard to feel bad for them. They refused to take the dangers seriously."

"I guess you're right, but it sounds pretty harsh."

John shrugged.

"Then again, you did everything you could to try to save them."

"Maybe I shouldn't have. We wouldn't be in this mess. We should have just run away."

"Maybe, maybe not."

Cynthia had tears in her eyes as she leaned in close. John smelled her breath, and he felt the warmth of her face as her cheek brushed against his. Their lips met, and they shared a brief kiss.

"What was that for?"

"I don't know. I'm going to go see if there's any water nearby."

"Be careful."

Cynthia patted the gun at her hip gently. "Don't worry. You've got yours?"

John nodded.

He watched Cynthia disappearing between the trees, water bottles dangling off of her pack.

For a few minutes, John was lost in thought. His thoughts, to his surprise, turned towards his pre-EMP life for the first time in a long time. Back then, he realized now, he had been a completely different person. It hadn't been that long, but he knew that the old John simply didn't exist anymore. He had been completely changed, becoming something that he never would have dreamed of.

John was proud of who he'd become. He'd learned along the way, and he'd been resourceful when it had counted. He'd become a person who was willing to do what needed to be done, and to learn new skills when necessary. He and Cynthia had stuck out the firearm thing, and somehow managed to teach themselves to be reasonable shooters, even conscious of gun safety.

When he thought of who he'd been before, he felt more embarrassed and ashamed than anything else. It hadn't been any way to live his life. He'd been screwing people over, one-upping everyone he could. And it had all been perfectly legal. He'd been chasing after nothing but status. He'd wanted to get ahead, to beat everyone he could. But it'd been nothing more than a race to absolutely nothing. Those numbers in the bank account meant nothing now. It had all come crashing down, and the social order had been completely upturned. John thought of his well-off acquaintances in Center City. No doubt they were long dead, having suffered horrible fates in their fancy downtown apartments.

Only those who'd been prepared, or those who were willing to do what was necessary—those were people who'd survive. Including, of course, a fair amount of luck.

Maybe the EMP had forced John to become the sort of person that he could have become, if he hadn't taken a different path since childhood. When he and his brother Max had been kids, they'd been so similar people couldn't even tell them apart. They'd done everything together, and then John had started to get ambitious, and sort of gone his own way. Maybe John had "regressed" in a way, but in a good way. Whatever. It was too complicated to think about. All he knew for certain was that he was becoming more like Max. And that was a good thing.

Something bustled in the bushes off to John's left.

He didn't even think about it—he reached for his gun

and moved himself into a more favorable shooting position.

He was ready for anything. Mentally, at least. His body still needed to recuperate.

He no longer felt that terror that he'd felt when first escaping the city. He knew how to act. He knew that if there was someone out there now, he'd be able to fight to defend himself. He'd do the best he could, and there wasn't any more that he could do. No point in worrying about it.

That didn't mean his blood didn't turn cold and his heart didn't start beating fast. It just meant he knew how to deal with those symptoms.

He took a deep breath and steadied his gun.

Another rustling in the bushes.

He saw them moving.

"Cynthia?" he called out.

No answer.

John waited. If it was someone, they knew he was there.

Suddenly, movement. The branches moved.

A rabbit jumped out from the bush. It seemed to see John, and it paused, frozen on the ground.

John breathed out a sigh of relief. It was just a rabbit. Just a cute little rabbit, rather than an orange-suited, gun-wielding, vicious criminal.

But it was more than just a cute little rabbit. It was large, quite plump. Pretty juicy looking, especially when John hadn't had a proper meal in who knew how long.

John aimed at the rabbit and squeezed the trigger.

The bullet hit the rabbit in the hindquarters, which was a shame, since that was where a lot of the good meat would be.

The rabbit lay motionless.

John re-holstered his gun, and struggled to his feet to examine the rabbit. With the promise of fresh meat to cook and eat, John somehow found the strength to stand.

He hobbled over weakly to the rabbit and bent down to examine it.

"Are you OK?" came Cynthia's voice, worried, as she crashed loudly into the little clearing.

"I'm fine," said John.

"I heard a gunshot... I thought the worst."

"Don't worry any longer. I just got us dinner."

Cynthia came over, a smile on her face. "You know, I had a pet rabbit as a kid. Normally it'd turn my stomach, seeing this. But I don't even care."

"I have a feeling I'll be feeling pretty good after eating this."

"Looks like your aim could have been a little better, though."

She pointed to where the bullet had destroyed a good bit of the meat.

"Yeah, I guess you're supposed to go rabbit hunting with smaller caliber bullets."

"Whatever, it'll still be delicious."

"Did you find any water, by the way?"

"Not yet."

"Give me a hand?"

John was starting to wobble a little, having trouble remaining in the crouching position.

Cynthia put her hand on his shoulder, but it didn't help. It knocked him a little more off balance, and he fell onto the ground again.

"You OK?" said Cynthia, bending down.

"I'm fine," said John, starting to laugh.

"You hit your head or something? Why are you laughing?"

"I don't know. Don't worry, I haven't lost it or anything. I just... I don't know."

John didn't want to admit it, but he felt happy. Maybe it was the rabbit. Maybe it was Cynthia. Maybe it was recognizing that he'd undergone some kind of transformation.

"Come on, I'm going to get this rabbit started. I figure we can risk a fire, right?"

"I don't see how we can avoid it. Not with this rabbit."

"I know, my mouth is already watering."

"We'll have to be extra careful, though. A fire might attract someone."

"We'll have to stay ready."

"You mean the guns?"

"Of course I mean the guns."

John was too tired to be of much good, but he helped Cynthia by telling her how to get the fire started.

"Keep the knife folded," said John, as Cynthia unfolded one of the pocket knives. "Just leave the blade in there. It's a lot safer that way, compared to having a long cutting edge out."

"OK, now what?"

"Just strike the flint across the back of the blade. Do it fast, with a bit of force. There you go, that's good."

"I don't think it's still called a flint. That was like forever ago."

"Well, whatever it is, it still works like a flint."

Cynthia was getting some good sparks, and soon the tinder they'd picked up days ago was lit.

"Quick," said John. "Get that tiny kindling on it."

"Easier said than done. All you have to do is sit there."

"I know. I could get used to this."

"Don't joke about that. Or you'll end up acting just like my husband."

It was the first time that Cynthia had mentioned her husband, now dead, in a long time. Or maybe she'd never mentioned him. John couldn't remember. But he did clearly remember the sight of his dead body in Cynthia's front yard, when he'd been on his way up to Valley Forge Park.

It felt like such a long time ago.

Did Cynthia still think of her husband?

Maybe things hadn't been that great between them, judging by what she was saying now. Not that it meant she was happy to see him go. She'd sobbed like crazy, after all.

Soon, there was a little fire roaring, and John was feeling good enough to sharpen up a spit for the rabbit.

The spit was easy in comparison to getting the rabbit ready to eat.

"I can't believe how much fur is on this thing," said Cynthia.

John laughed. "What did you expect? It's covered in fur."

"I guess the real problem is I don't have any idea what I'm doing."

"Just don't think of your pet rabbit."

"Jerk," said Cynthia, laughing, kicking a little bit of dirt up at him with her boot.

Suddenly, John had a bad feeling in the pit of his stomach.

"You know," he said. "Things are..."

"What?"

"Going good."

"You sound like that's not a good thing."

"It just has me worried. How often do we laugh?"

"Basically never. I figure we're just happy to have some meat to eat soon."

"I don't know…"

"It's been less than an hour. No need to worry. I'm sure things will go to shit soon enough."

25

MILLER

It was quiet for a while. He heard their boots moving on the hardwood floor outside. For the moment, they'd stopped attacking the door. He couldn't remember how many there'd been. The adrenaline should have made his mind sharp. But it was foggy. Maybe it was the pain from the gunshot wound. Maybe it was the stress. Maybe it was something else.

Miller didn't regret anything. He didn't regret the fact that he was going to die. He'd taken some of them out. That was what he wanted.

If there was a shred of regret, it was that he hadn't thought about his plan more, and gotten to the leader. But it was unrealistic. He should have known that. He would have never gotten there.

His plan had sounded like something from a spy novel, not something from real life.

He'd done what he could.

These hadn't been the men who'd killed his wife and son. But they were close enough. They were cut from the same cloth, so to speak. They were part of the same organization.

They started again.

Miller was reeling in pain. But he stood tall and strong.

Bullets sprang through the thin wooden door.

The door was shaking with kicks. And body slams. They were throwing their bodies against it.

The dresser couldn't hold out much more, and Miller couldn't get close enough to hold it back, unless he wanted to take another bullet.

Finally, the dresser had danced back a bit from the door, from the impacts.

A heavy boot broke through the door, splintered wood going everywhere. A hand reached through, going for the doorknob. The weight of the dresser was enough to keep the door mostly in its frame.

Miller aimed carefully, squeezing the trigger.

A howl of pain. The hand retreated, bloodied. He'd shot good. But it wouldn't be enough.

It happened so fast it was hard to register it all. The door was opened, the dresser kicked back.

One of them entered. He knew where Miller would be. His face was contorted in rage. His hand was bloodied. He had his gun in his other hand.

He and Miller shot at the same time.

The guy went down, thrown back a little.

Miller took the bullet in the chest. His breathing was going all funny. He felt the blood pooling.

These would be some of his last moments. He wasn't going to make it.

But he was going to take out the last one.

Or were there two?

He couldn't think straight. His mind was a mess of adrenaline and pain. Everything was confusing.

The only thing he could do to steady himself was keep the grip on his gun tight. And his finger on the trigger.

More movement.

Someone else came through the door.

Miller had his gun on him.

But the other guy was too fast.

Miller saw everything in slow motion. But his own reactions were too slow. The guy pulled the trigger.

Miller felt the bullet hit the center of his chest.

He had several seconds of consciousness before he died. Nothing but a flash of his past memories, playing in his mind's eye. Like he was watching a film, surprisingly clear, but as if he was peering down onto everything. He felt close to the events, but far away at the same time.

His son's first birthday party. His wife was sobbing in the kitchen, because none of their friends had even bothered to respond to the invitations. And no one had showed up. The balloons hung sadly up around the ceiling.

The first time he'd met his wife. That tight sweater she'd been wearing in the dead of winter, when the sun never seemed to rise high enough to burn off the winter doldrums.

Miller's first day of kindergarten, when he'd been a boisterous kid full of energy, ready to cause havoc, ready to make the kindergarten teacher cry.

The little film cut off suddenly. Miller knew no more.

26

GEORGIA

"Did you hear that?" said Mandy.

Georgia nodded.

It had been the unmistakable sound of a gun going off. A handgun, by the sound of it.

"What do we do?"

Georgia didn't answer. She was worried about their safety and their future. Most of all, she was worried about her daughter. What Kara had described wasn't any kind of life. It'd be a life of confinement and unparalleled misery.

They needed to get out of there.

"If only Max were here."

"We can't rely on Max now. We've got to work this out ourselves. You still have your knife, right?"

Mandy nodded, patting her cheap utility knife in its sheath.

"Good."

Georgia took out her own knife, a Buck 110. It was big and heavy, but in reality the clip point blade wasn't that long. The Mora blade might have been longer. It'd work, though, in a pinch. It had a solid lockup, and Georgia felt fairly confident it'd function as a weapon without the lock folding and the blade snapping closed on her fingers.

"What are we going to do, Mom?"

"We're going to fight."

"Without guns?"

"There aren't any other options. We're going to have to fight our way out. We can't stay here."

"What about James?"

"We're going to try to find him. James can take care of himself."

"Do you think he'll come looking for us?"

"Definitely."

Georgia didn't want to admit it out loud, but she was worried that James was going to get himself killed trying to get them out of there. Once he got wind of the plan, there was no way he would stand for it. But he was still smaller than an adult, and weaker. He'd grow into a man one day, hopefully, but he wasn't yet there yet. He wasn't a match for the men here.

"Do you hear that?" whispered Mandy.

Georgia heard it. There were footsteps right outside the door. They weren't heavy.

Georgia knew those footsteps.

"James?" she called out, hoping against hope that she wasn't wrong.

"Mom?"

"James! Can you get the lock?"

"What's happening, James?" said Sadie.

"There's no time for that," said Georgia, thinking practically. "Can you open the lock?"

"I don't have a key."

"What do you have?"

"A handgun. From a dead guy. They took my bullets. I don't have much time."

"OK, shoot the lock. Do it at an angle so that there's no risk of it ricocheting off and hitting you."

James said nothing.

But a moment later, there was a gunshot.

"James?"

"One second."

She heard James pulling the busted lock off of the door.

The next thing she knew, James had thrown the door open. He stood tall in the doorway, looking more like a man than ever before. There was blood on him.

"Have you been shot? Are you injured?"

James shook his head.

There wasn't time for him to tell them what had happened. But it was there in his eyes—something had happened, for sure.

"They'll be coming. They'll have heard the gunshot."

Georgia turned to see Mandy already grabbing her gear.

"Sadie, get your stuff. Quick. James, stay outside. Shoot anyone who comes."

"Where's Chad?" said Mandy.

"He didn't make it."

No one said anything. They were rushing for their gear.

Georgia hated to keep James outside like that, exposed to anything that might come his way. She feared a bullet might lodge itself in James's chest. The only thing that was protecting him now was the mild darkness of the compound. There were some ambient lights—powered by a battery that had been protected during the EMP—and lights from the building, that gave more background light than you'd find in the depths of the woods.

In mere moments, they had most of their stuff.

James stuck his head inside.

"We're going to have a hard time getting out of here. I see them, off on the other side. They're grouping up. Or waiting."

"I know."

"What's the plan then, Mom?"

Georgia didn't know. She didn't see how they could possibly get out.

There were concrete walls they'd have to scale. And there were people on watch all over. They'd never get all of the group safely over the walls.

Getting through the front gate would be problematic, to say the least. There was a guard always there.

The real problem was that the compound wasn't that large. And there were a lot of people in it.

There wasn't really anywhere to hide.

They were going to have to try, though. There wasn't anything else to do. Staying wasn't an option. She wouldn't let Mandy or her daughter go through that, no matter how far down the road it was. The threat was simply too serious.

"Everyone ready?"

"Yeah."

"Did they take your ammo too?" said James.

"Yeah."

"Here, Mom," said James, handing the handgun to Georgia. "You should have this. You can use it better than any of us."

Georgia took it. She handed her Buck knife to James.

"Everyone have a knife?"

They all nodded, and showed their knives.

Sadie looked terrified, but there wasn't any time to comfort her.

"Just so everyone knows," blurted out James, suddenly, as they all filed through the doorway. "Chad tried to save me. It was the last thing he did."

Georgia knew there was something else that James wasn't telling them. But it wasn't the time to delve into that now. Maybe never.

"We'll head into the shadows, between the buildings," whispered Georgia.

She kept the handgun ready, as she led everyone, single file, out into the shadows.

They were just in time.

There were footsteps coming. Heavy boots. Lots of men. No way to tell how many. Frantic whispers and commands.

Georgia realized they'd be pursued. They couldn't hide long.

She stopped. "We're going to have to head out the gate. It's going to be dangerous. But there's no other way."

The cars, everyone knew, were outside the concrete walls. Georgia felt for the keys in her pocket. They were still there. Max had the other set.

Where was Max?

No time for that now.

"We'll never make it out," said Mandy.

"We've got to try."

"We're talking about the lives of your kids here. And ours too."

They were talking in hushed whispers, in the shadows. The concrete walls were on either side, creating a narrow alley. It was as if they were prisoners of war. The once-inviting compound had transformed into a prison camp.

"It's better than the alternative. We've got to get out. Or die trying."

Georgia gritted her teeth to prevent tears forming in her eyes.

"You go ahead," she said to Mandy. "James and Sadie, follow Mandy. I'll take up the rear. I've got the one working gun. Use your rifles as clubs. Use your knives."

"Mom..." said Sadie, tugging on Georgia's sleeve.

"Go!" hissed Georgia.

A single tear managed to escape her eye, but no one saw it. They were already heading through the dark corridor between the barracks.

The front gate was maybe 100 feet down in that direction, off to the side.

"They're over there!"

"I see one!"

The shouts from the men were coming. They weren't trying to be quiet now. They were shouting, murmuring, their boots stomping. They had become an angry mob, intent on taking the women back.

A single female voice rang out above the male voices. It was Kara. "Don't let them escape!" shouted Kara. There was an edge to her voice, a viciousness.

Georgia turned to look, just barely seeing Sadie's back as she followed her brother.

Georgia knelt down, turning back to the direction the mob was coming from. She checked the pistol first.

It was a six shooter, unknown make. Seemed good enough, though. High caliber bullets. Good stopping power, probably good accuracy. Hopefully, at least. But still, it wasn't the sort of gun Georgia would have chosen if she'd had the option.

But she didn't.

The shouts were closer.

Georgia got as close to the concrete wall as she could.

A small guy rounded the corner. He was the first, but he wouldn't be the last.

"They're heading towards the gate!"

He saw Georgia too late. He pointed his gun.

Georgia took aim, squeezed the trigger.

The kickback felt good in her hands. It felt like she was doing something, taking some action.

The roar of the gun was deafening. Nothing she wasn't used to, though. Not at this point.

Her shot hit him in the head. His body crumpled to the ground.

One more, thought Georgia. Maybe two.

She'd make a last stand if she had to. If it meant Sadie and James getting out alive.

But they'd need her help. They had no weapons. It'd be better if she could join them.

And she didn't want to die.

Two rounded the corner.

Georgia squeezed the trigger. She aimed. Squeezed the trigger again.

Two down in quick succession. A pile of bodies. Georgia didn't even look.

Three bullets used. Two more left.

Georgia made her move. It was time.

She sprang up and dashed down toward the gate, where her children and Mandy had headed.

She didn't look back. She ran with all her might, her legs churning under her, just like she'd done when running track in high school. She'd been one of the fastest. But that was years ago.

She heard the bullets. They hit the concrete, sending shards into her face.

She heard the footsteps behind her. Dozens of them. Heavy boots.

She heard the shouting.

Up ahead, she saw her children and Mandy dashing towards the guardhouse.

There were two guards, emerging now from the little guardhouse.

They held handguns, pointing them at Mandy and James and Sadie.

There'd be no way to get past them, not with the wooden gate blocking the exit. It was shut, and padlocked, as Kara had explained was the custom at night.

Georgia didn't have time to think.

There wasn't time to reach them. She'd have to make the shot from here.

And it meant getting shot herself. Most likely.

Georgia stopped in her tracks, raised her gun. She took a moment to take careful aim. It was too long, putting her in danger. After all, they were chasing her down from behind. She shouldn't have stopped like that. But it was what she had to do.

It was almost too far to take the shot. But Georgia was good. She could do it.

The gun kicked, and she saw the guard fall.

The other guard looked up, but it was too late for him.

Georgia aimed at him, squeezed the trigger, and he fell.

It'd been a hard shot, but she'd done it. Her kids had a chance of escaping now.

Georgia felt the bullet hit her back. Pain roared through her. But she didn't fall. She staggered forward. Her gun fell from her hand, making a heavy thud on the ground.

"Mom!" cried out Sadie, turning around, staring down the corridor between the barracks.

27

JOHN

"You feeling better?"

John nodded. His mouth was full of roasted rabbit. He didn't care about opening his mouth when he spoke, but he did care about losing an opportunity to continue eating the rabbit. Time with his mouth open meant time spent talking rather than chewing. He wanted to get it all inside him, as much of the rabbit as he could.

"I can't believe how well this turned out," said Cynthia. "Here, have the rest of mine."

John shook his head. He couldn't take her food. Food was life now.

"Seriously, take it. You're not looking that much better."

John accepted the legs she handed him. There was a bit of fur on one of them still. It'd been harder to get it off then they'd thought. They'd done quite a number on the rabbit, definitely butchering it in a completely incorrect way. But, whatever, it had worked, and it was cooked and they could eat it. That was the important thing.

A bit of fur didn't bother him. He just picked it off when he could. Or he'd pick it out of his teeth later. It didn't matter.

"You need it, trust me. You look terrible."

"I get the point," said John, finally speaking.

"So you can talk. The rumors are true."

John nodded vigorously instead of laughing.

"Did you hear that?"

"What?"

John used the opportunity of his open mouth to take another huge bite of rabbit leg, tearing the meat right off the bone with his teeth. He'd never even eaten rabbit before now. Not once. It wasn't like it was often on the menu at the places he'd frequented before the EMP.

"You don't hear it?"

John shook his head. But he put his rabbit meat down carefully on the ground. He looked around, but he didn't see anything.

A split second later, something came running into their little camp.

It was a huge furry dog, a German Shepherd, tan and black, with pointed ears.

John pulled out his gun.

"What are you doing?" cried Cynthia. "You can't shoot it."

John had never been an animal lover, but on the same token he wasn't going to relish shooting a dog. But if it was a danger to them, he wouldn't hesitate.

The dog didn't seem interested in attacking them. Instead, it went straight for John's rabbit meat.

"No!" shouted John, swatting at the dog's face and pulling the meat back up into his arms.

The dog sat down, obediently, as if it had been given a

command. It looked up at John with pleading eyes, patiently waiting.

Cynthia started laughing. "It just wants a little rabbit. Can you blame it? It must have smelled it."

John didn't laugh. Instead, he cast his gaze around into the surrounding trees.

"Someone's here," he whispered.

Cynthia's hand went to her own gun.

"How do you know?"

"This dog is trained. It's someone's dog."

"Maybe he's on his own. His owner might have died."

"Look at him. He's clean and well fed."

Cynthia nodded, and stood up, ready to take action if needed.

"Kiki!" came someone's voice. A deep male voice.

The man emerged from behind the trees. He was tall, broad-shouldered, with a sizeable beard, trimmed. His hair was thick and streaked with gray, short, but wild-looking even so.

"Don't move!" shouted Cynthia, pointing her gun right at the man's chest.

John did the same, and he kept his eyes on the surrounding area, in case someone else appeared.

"Whoa, whoa!" said the man. "I'm just looking for my dog. Not looking for any trouble."

His voice was deep and pleasant, and it sounded trustworthy. Not that that was anything to go by.

"Who are you?" shouted Cynthia.

John and Cynthia had their guns trained on the guy, but he didn't look scared. The jovial expression didn't leave his face.

"Dale Baughner. I know, hard to pronounce. Most just call me The Bastard."

"The Bastard? What kind of a name is that?"

"Just a joke between me and my friends. Of course, I don't see them much these days." With that, he gave a deep laugh that came up from his stomach. "Don't worry, though. It wouldn't be a very good nickname if I really was a bastard. It's funny because I'm anything but."

"Are you armed?"

"Armed? Of course I'm armed. Don't you know what's happened?"

"What do you have?"

"Two pistols on me. And the rifle on my back, if you hadn't noticed."

John had been so overwhelmed that he hadn't noticed the rifle. He felt like an idiot. He saw it now, a well-worn strap over Dale's shoulder.

"What are you doing here?"

"Well, I was walking Kiki here. Surveying the land, you know. And Kiki must have smelled the rabbit you were roasting there. Normally she's very well behaved, but hell, I guess when there's rabbit involved, there's no telling her what to do. It's her instincts, you understand?"

Dale had an interesting, colloquial kind of way of talking. It made John feel like he already had known him for a while. He simply seemed to be the type of person who was always comfortable, no matter who he was talking to. He seemed sure of himself, more than most.

There wasn't a trace of fear in his voice. But John know that Dale wasn't the type to be oblivious to his surroundings. Beneath all that hair, partially hiding near the big beard, Dale's eyes were sharp. And they moved around, studying the little campsite that he and Cynthia had constructed.

"If you don't mind me asking," said Dale, in his great

scratching, booming voice. "What the hell happened to your shoulder there?"

"Little misunderstanding," said John. "It couldn't be helped."

"And what are you doing out in these parts?"

"Long story," said John.

"Very long," said Cynthia.

"Well," said Dale. "Tell you what. Why don't you two follow me and Kiki back to my cabin? It's nothing fancy, but I'll feed you some proper food. Believe it or not, there's better stuff out there than wild rabbit." He laughed, as if this was the funniest thing anyone had ever said. "Kind of tough unless you cook it the right way. Real gamey. Now I like it fine, but it's not normal for you city folks."

"How can you tell I'm from the city?"

"It's written all over you. I can read people just like you read the phonebook. Easy for me, always was. I can tell you're good people."

"How?"

"Well, for one thing, if you weren't, you'd have shot me by now. But here I am. Come on, put the guns down and let's get moving. You look like you could use a good place to rest for a couple days. Nothing permanent, understand? But I'd enjoy the company, to tell you the truth."

John glanced over at Cynthia. She raised one of her eyebrows, as if asking a question.

John gave her a little nod, and she gave him a smile. He could see in her eyes that she wasn't concerned that Dale would harm them. With some people, you just knew. There wasn't anything of the slick self-promotion that Drew exuded. People who wanted to trick others always gave themselves away, in some way, shape, or form. No matter how good they were, they'd always slip up, even in the tiniest way.

John re-holstered his gun, and Cynthia did the same.

"Now we're getting somewhere," said Dale, walking over and extending a hand to Cynthia and John each.

John and Cynthia introduced themselves, and Dale in turn introduced them to Kiki, his German Shepherd, who licked their hands and sat obediently.

"Maybe your new friends will give you some of the rabbit bones. What do you think, Kiki? They seem like nice people, right?"

"Sure," muttered John, taking one final bite off his rabbit leg and tossing the bone to Kiki. Kiki caught it mid-air.

"That a girl, Kiki," said Dale, laughing uproariously.

"We really appreciate the offer," said Cynthia. "About staying at your place. How far away is it, though? John here lost a lot of blood. He was lucky to live. I don't know if he'll be able to make it."

"About five miles away. But he'll make it, trust me. You're a strong one, aren't you? For a city guy, that is."

John didn't know what to say. He and Cynthia started gathering up their gear and getting ready to head off.

"I'd better take that pack of yours, though," said Dale. "You've still got your sea legs, so to speak."

"Uh, thanks," said John. He didn't relish the idea of another man, a stranger nonetheless, having to carry his pack for him, but he was pragmatic enough to realize that he needed the help.

"Come on," said Dale. "Let's get a move on it."

It was strange how much John and Cynthia already trusted Dale. But it would have been hard not to.

"You sure about this?" whispered Cynthia, as they

started off, Dale and Kiki plenty of paces ahead of them. "Can we really trust him?"

"Yeah," said John. "I'm good at reading people, too, just like him. There's just something about him."

"I get the same feeling," said Cynthia. "But what if we're wrong?"

"Don't worry, we're not. The only problem with him is that he talks really loud."

"What was that?" said Dale, loudly, turning his head around.

"Nothing," said John.

"There's one thing you should know about, though," called out Cynthia.

"What's that? You'd better come up here where I can hear you better. Come on, don't be shy."

Cynthia gave John a look that he didn't know how to interpret before speeding up and joining Dale.

"There are two men out there. Criminals, really nasty guys. They killed our two friends and stole their gear. They're armed now. Handguns. And plenty of ammunition. We don't know if they're still around here or not."

"Don't worry, little lady," said Dale. "I'll keep my eyes out, and Kiki never misses a beat. She can smell trouble a mile away."

John had his doubts about whether Kiki the German Shepherd would really be that much of a help, but on the other hand, three against two was better than two against two. And Dale had an air about him like that of the old solitary mountain men—in some way, at least. John had the feeling that Dale knew his away around a gun pretty well.

John was already feeling weak again. He could probably make the five miles, but it would be tough on him.

He was short of breath, and he stopped for a moment, taking in deep breaths of the fresh air. He glanced up at the sun, which was high in the sky.

Fall had come, and John and Cynthia hadn't even noticed. They weren't yet into those seriously cold months, but they would be coming soon.

What would happen if they went west? Where would they go? Would they be able to hack it if they went north, into colder climates? What about nudging the course a little to the south, to avoid the freezing temperatures of the other states? Wouldn't more people be headed in the same direction? More people meant more problems. There'd be others like John and Cynthia, looking for the same thing, looking for shelter from the storm, a place to ride out the waves of a crumbling civilization.

Dale's cabin sounded like an enticing respite from the violence and pain they'd endured. But it wasn't the end. If John and Cynthia managed to live, they'd look back at this and realize that Dale's cabin was only the beginning of a long journey. But from where John stood now, it seemed like the end. It made him feel weak, down to his bones, to think about continuing on and on, without break, relentlessly fighting the tides of humanity that washed over them.

"You feeling alright?" called Cynthia, turning around. She and Dale had gotten pretty far ahead of him.

"Come on, buddy," called out Dale. "We want to get there before next week. You're not that bad off, come on."

John felt with the palm of his hand the reassuring weight of his handgun, and started off again.

28

MAX

It had taken Max a long time to hotwire the Bronco. For some reason, Mandy had needed the keys to the Honda that he'd been driving. Maybe she'd gone to get something out of it. Max couldn't remember. Georgia had the keys to the Bronco.

The Bronco and the Honda were parked close to the compound. The concrete walls were close, and there'd been murmurs of sounds coming out of the compound.

He'd known the Bronco would be easier to hotwire. It was far older than the Honda, and hopefully less sophisticated.

Max had broken the window of the Bronco with a small rock. He'd held his breath, hoping that the noise wouldn't be enough to alert anyone to his presence. No one had come running out of the compound. Max would have been ready if they had. He wouldn't have hesitated to use deadly force again. Not with what was at stake.

Like most people, Max had never hotwired anything in his life. He understood the basic theory. The way he saw it, he'd open the area beneath the steering wheel, and connect wires until something happened.

It had worked, but it had taken Max a long time.

He'd heard the first gunshot, and he'd known that his friends needed help. Desperately. But there wasn't anything he could do but keep his head down and keep connecting wires together until something happened.

He'd heard the second gunshot, and then another.

He hoped that it wasn't already too late.

Max was sweating as he finally got the Bronco to start. The engine roared to life, chugging along obediently.

More gunshots. Loud in the cold, dark night.

Max didn't hesitate. He jammed the Bronco into first and drove in a small circle, giving himself some space to get up to speed.

He hit second gear.

Now third.

He was going about 40MPH. He didn't look at the dashboard, though. His eyes were fixed on the wooden door. On the other side, there'd be the guardhouse. Men with guns, ready to shoot him.

Max didn't know what awaited him on the other side of that wood.

But he knew he had to drive through it.

He might get shot instantly. His act might not accomplish anything.

He would have preferred a subtler method for getting his friends out. But the gunshots he'd heard told him there wasn't much time left. If there was any time left at all.

He had to take the chance.

The Bronco hit the wood with a jolt, crashing right through it.

Some of the wood splintered. Mostly the whole door got flattened by the Bronco.

Max didn't have time to analyze exactly what had happened. He kept his foot on the accelerator, pressing down as hard as he could.

The door had slowed him down, but he drove into the compound fast.

Gunshots, loud, unmistakable even over the deep roar of the Bronco's engine.

Max's eyes darted around the compound, looking for the source of the gunshots, looking for his friends.

He saw them. Some of them at least. Maybe the rest were out of view. They were huddled inside the little guard station.

Max slammed on the brakes. The Bronco came to such an abrupt halt that Max slammed into the steering wheel, awakening old injuries and bruises. Pain flared through his body. After all, he'd never had the chance to heal properly.

Mandy's head appeared above some wood of the guard structure, a handgun held straight, releasing rounds.

It seemed like bullets were coming from all directions. But they were sporadic. Hard to tell where they were coming from. The enemies were far away. For now. As far as they could be in a confined compound.

Bullets hit the Bronco. One hit the window, going right through it, lodging itself somewhere in the Bronco's faded upholstery. A spiderweb of shattered glass stayed miraculously in place on the windshield.

Then Max saw it.

Georgia. Down a corridor between two concrete buildings. Halfway hidden in the dark.

She was running. But not very well. She was hurt. And hurt bad.

Men were behind her, shooting.

Another bullet went through the Bronco's windshield.

Max ignored it.

Max threw open the door of the Bronco and jumped out. His leg flared with pain as he hit the ground.

He'd stopped the Bronco close enough to the guard structure that the door provided some cover for Mandy and the others.

"Is everyone here?"

"Everyone except Georgia," shouted Mandy.

"Get in! And get down! Return fire when it's safe."

Max was in the guard structure. He grabbed Sadie from the ground and carried her into the Bronco. She was sobbing.

He practically threw her in.

"Keep her on the floor in the back!" he shouted at Mandy.

Mandy nodded.

"James!"

James was next, moving on his own into the Bronco.

The enemies were staying back, out of sight, hidden in the dark shadows of the cold concrete buildings. They were clever. The worst kind of enemy.

Max was crouched behind the open door. He surveyed the group in the car. Mandy, Sadie, and James were all there.

"Where's Chad?"

"Dead."

Max felt like he'd received a blow in the stomach. But he said nothing.

"Get my mom!" sobbed Sadie, completely uncontrolled wailing issuing forth from her shaking body.

Georgia was close. Not close enough, though.

Max needed a plan. But he didn't have time to come up with one.

Max threw himself into the Bronco's driver seat.

Max gunned the engine, threw it into first, foot depressing the gas pedal, releasing the clutch with a jerk, and the Bronco rocketed forward towards Georgia.

Georgia was in the shadows. She'd gotten behind a piece of the concrete structure that jutted out, shielding her momentarily from the gunshots of the people behind her in the corridor. She was returning fire, keeping them at bay.

Max drove the Bronco fast towards the entrance to the corridor. Georgia was maybe ten feet down inside it.

Georgia couldn't make the rest of the way herself. Not without some cover fire. If she stopped returning fire herself, they'd have a clear shot at her as she ran the rest of the way.

Max slammed on the brakes, the Bronco skidding to a stop, kicking up the dry dirt from the compound ground.

Max had his Glock out the window, returning fire. His finger felt good on the trigger, squeezing. He felt a thrill rush through him. He felt alive, energized. All his pain lay in the background, dormant, forgotten. Adrenaline was his king, his motivator.

"If we return fire, she'll be able to make it."

Mandy took the cue. She used their one other gun to fire out the window, towards the men at the other end of the corridor. So did James.

Georgia turned briefly in the darkness.

"She sees us. She'll make a run for it."

"Come on, Mom," muttered James, from the back.

Max saw some movement off to his side. Almost too late. But not quite.

It was a guy aiming a rifle at them. He'd snuck up from somewhere.

Max's arm moved fast. He released a string of bullets. One of them hit the guy. He went down.

More would come. They were all over the place. Not just down the corridor. They didn't have much time. They needed to get out of there.

Max turned back to Georgia.

Her face was in the darkness. He couldn't see her expression.

But he saw her keel over, falling hard to the ground. The gun dropped from her hand.

Sadie screamed.

James made a noise of pain.

Max didn't think about it. He just acted.

Georgia wasn't getting out of there herself.

"I'm going in. Cover me, or we'll never get out of there."

"Max! You can't go." Frantic worry dripped over Mandy's words.

"There's no time."

Max opened his door.

"I'll go down the left side. Shoot to the right."

Max would have to rely on the accuracy of Mandy and James. A single stray bullet and he'd take one in the back.

Max sprinted towards Georgia. He ran in a lopsided way. His leg had never properly healed. Pain, and more pain. The adrenaline couldn't keep it off. But he ran. He held the Glock in front of him, squeezing the trigger indiscriminately until he was out of ammo.

He didn't pay attention to the gunfire around him. Mandy and James would do everything they could. No point in worrying about it. He'd either get shot or he wouldn't.

He was ready for anything.

"Georgia!"

She was out, her limbs akimbo on the ground.

Max shook her, trying to keep against the wall as best he could, a slim profile for the shooters.

Georgia didn't respond. Max felt for a pulse. It was there. Weak, but it was still there. She was still alive. But she wasn't getting out of there on her own legs.

Max grabbed her and strained as he picked her up. His leg was on fire.

He turned and started back to the Bronco.

He kept to the side as best he could. Bullets whizzed by him. Muzzle flashes up ahead. Mandy and James were doing a hell of a job keeping up the gunfire. So long as one of their bullets didn't go astray...

Max didn't think about any of that. He didn't think about his leg. Or how close to death he was. He thought about the Bronco, getting there. That was it.

Somehow, he made it. Just when he thought he couldn't take another step with Georgia's weight applying so much force to his leg.

James had the back door open already and Max set Georgia's body down roughly on the backseat.

A bullet hit the open door. Better to go in through the back than risk getting into the driver's seat from the outside.

Max threw himself over Georgia's body, jamming himself between James, Sadie, and Georgia.

"Get us out of here," barked Max.

Mandy was already sliding over to the driver's seat. She had the Bronco in reverse, and sent them speeding backwards with a jolt that threw Max into the seat.

Mandy spun the wheel and threw the Bronco into a sharp turn. Dirt was up around them, dust. Good, it would help obscure them. Better cover.

In a flash, Mandy had it in first. They were hurtling forward, right toward the door Max had flattened on his way in.

"There's someone in the way!" shouted Mandy.

A man with a gun stood in their path. A shotgun in his hands. Ready to unload.

The Bronco sped towards him.

The man lowered the shotgun.

"Go!" shouted Max. "Go!"

Sadie screamed as Mandy kept her foot on the pedal and flattened the guy. The Bronco bumped over his body, one side of the vehicle going up and down again. A sickening thud underneath the chassis.

But they were out. They were safe, for the moment.

But there was no time to celebrate their victory. Georgia was unconscious, her breathing shallow.

And they were out, speeding away from the compound.

Max had Georgia in his arms, his fingers pressed to her neck.

"She's still with us. But she's badly hurt. Get her shirt off. We need to find the wound."

James had a pocket knife out and started cutting away Georgia's shirt. A grim look had overtaken his face.

The shirt was colored a deep red with blood. James's hands, when he took them away, were soaked in blood.

"I don't see it."

"Help me get her on her stomach. Sadie, get into the front with Mandy. We need space."

"Come on, Sadie," said James, tugging on his sobbing sister, basically pulling and pushing her until she was in the front seat, from which she peered back with anxious terror.

Max and James got Georgia onto her stomach.

"She's been shot. It missed her spine. Let's hope it didn't puncture her lungs."

Max knew that if Georgia's lungs had taken the bullet, there'd be no way to save her.

Even if she'd gotten lucky, she'd be lucky to live. The bullet hadn't exited. It was still lodged inside her.

29

JOHN

"That walk really took it out of you, didn't it?" said Dale boisterously. He seemed to have gotten even more energized the closer he'd gotten to his little cabin.

"I'm... OK..." John managed to say. He threw himself to the ground and tried to catch his breath. But he was still weak, and his breaths were shallow, as if his lungs weren't getting the air they needed.

"You did good," said Cynthia, putting a comforting hand on his shoulder. "Can you make it inside?"

John nodded, and held up a finger, indicating he needed some more time to rest.

In front of John sat Dale's little wooden cabin. It was picturesque, surrounded by tall evergreen trees, nestled perfectly in the woods. A chimney was perched on the roof. Wisps of smoke escaped it.

The scene looked like something out of a fairytale. Who was this man, Dale? He lived like a woodsman alone in the woods, in a log cabin that he surely must have built himself.

"I'll get the teakettle going," said Dale. "Don't worry, honey, he'll be fine in a jiffy. I've seen men lose plenty of blood before. He'll be fine."

John didn't feel like he'd been fine. His body felt so weak he couldn't even make it the few steps into the cabin, into which Dale now disappeared.

"You'll be fine," said Cynthia, her voice soft. "Just hang in there. Don't die on me and leave me alone with Dale. I have a feeling he likes to talk a lot."

John gave a weak little laugh. Cynthia had a way of cheering him up in the strangest ways possible.

After a few minutes, John was feeling better. He felt his strength returning, little by little, warming up his muscles that had felt dead just minutes earlier. It was amazing the abuse the human body could take, and what it could come back from.

"It's nice here," said John, finally catching his breath enough to speak a little.

"Yeah," said Cynthia, looking around. "If the EMP hadn't happened, this is the sort of spot people would pay a lot of money to come and vacation at."

John chuckled weakly. "I was never one for the great outdoors myself. Preferred New York City. Ritz Carlton, the Met, places like that."

"You were one of those types. Don't worry, I've already got you all figured out. But you're a changed man now."

"I'm learning to enjoy the little things. Like having a bullet just graze me, instead of lodging inside me."

Cynthia laughed.

"I certainly didn't take any vacations to New York City, but I wasn't the type for the outdoors either."

"What'd you do then?"

"Oh, not much. Watch movies, stay in, stuff like that."

"Sounds fun."

"I thought it was, but I didn't know what I was missing."

"You'd prefer this life?"

Cynthia laughed. "I'm not saying that. But there is something about this. I feel... more free than I did before the EMP, trapped inside, the television always on. I wasn't really living."

"Yeah," said John. "Nothing to make you feel like you're really alive than getting shot and attacked all the time."

"I'm not saying this is better, but you know what I mean."

"I think so. Come on, I'm ready to go inside."

"You folks going to join me or what?" shouted Dale, poking his head out the quaint front door.

"We're on our way," said Cynthia.

She helped John to his feet, supporting a lot of his weight.

"I can make it on my own," said John, wincing a little as he started towards the cabin.

It wasn't a long way. Not by any stretch of the imagination. A mere handful of paces. Too close for Dale to shout. But he had a habit of communicating loudly.

And, as John and Cynthia soon found out, Dale had a habit of doing everything loudly.

They joined him inside, and he was busy by the wood stove, making a hell of a racket with a collection of cast iron pots and pans that he banged around.

The cabin was small, somewhat cramped with the three of them in there. But there were three chairs, and they were comfortable. Or at least comfortable compared to simply sitting on the ground, as John and Cynthia had been doing since they'd left the farmhouse. In fact, they'd spent most of their time since the EMP sitting or lying on the hard ground. In comparison, the chairs felt incredible.

"These are amazing chairs," said Cynthia.

Dale was pouring hot water into three separate mugs.

"Nothing fancy," said Dale. "Made them myself."

"Did you make the whole cabin?"

"Yup. And a lot of what's in it. All the wood stuff, mostly."

John accepted a mug from Dale, who'd added a metal infuser filled with loose tea.

The liquid was hot enough to give off some steam, and it felt comforting to hold it in both his hands.

"Give it a minute to steep properly," said Dale.

"We're lucky we came across you," said John, suddenly realizing just how lucky they were to find themselves in a comfortable home, resting, drinking real tea.

"Thank Kiki," said Dale. "Or thank that rabbit."

Kiki was sitting obediently on the floor, curled up.

"Now," said Dale, sitting down across from John and Cynthia, with his own mug. "I've got some sausages we can have soon. But I figure your stomachs have shrunk down a bit over the weeks, and that rabbit filled them up pretty good. So I'll wait a while on that."

"Sounds good," said John. "I'm not hungry yet, but I know I'll be pretty hungry when I am."

Dale laughed.

He seemed almost too good-natured.

"I've got to thank you," said John. "You're being really... almost too hospitable to us."

"It's the least I can do," said Dale. "I could see you're two decent people. And sounds like you've been through hell."

"Pretty much, yeah. What about you? How've you been weathering the post-EMP world?"

"Not too bad, really," said Dale, kicking his feet up on a small wooden stool, and taking a sip of his tea. "I've had this place for ages, and it's got just about all I could need."

"You lived here before the EMP?"

"Yup, about ten years. I was never the type for cities or anything like that. Always liked to be on my own, mostly. Of course, I had some friends around. People who'd stop by once in a while when they're on hunting trips. And there's a town about forty miles away I'd stop into once in a while, pick up supplies and that sort of thing."

"Wait," said Cynthia. "So your life is basically unchanged since the EMP? I mean, this is how you've been living for ten years? This place doesn't even look like it's wired for electricity. You're definitely not on the grid."

"Nope," said Dale, laughing. "That's the way I always preferred it. Simpler. And cheaper. I used to drive trucks, but I got tired of it. Made enough money I could buy this little piece of land here, with nothing around it for miles. Seemed to suit me just fine. So I took my time and built the place the way I wanted it."

"Your friends," said John, "what happened to them?"

"Well, no one's been stopping by, that's for sure. I imagine they've got their own problems now. No chance to go on hunting trips for vacation. People used to come from all over. I was bound to see someone at least once a week."

"What about the town?"

"Haven't been back yet," said Dale. "Truth is, I'm a little scared of what I might find. Lots of people don't stock up the way I do, and I don't have enough to help others. Except for the occasional meal, of course. Don't worry, you're no imposition or anything like that. I wouldn't have offered if I couldn't dish up when the time came." That sent him laughing again.

He seemed fine with his life since the EMP. In a sense, at least.

"Aren't you worried about your own safety?" said John. "The tea is delicious, by the way."

"Yup," said Dale. "It's good stuff. What do you mean by worried?"

"Well, right now there are those two criminals we told you about. They're out there, armed, and they won't hesitate to kill."

Dale laughed. "The thing about people like that is that they never seem to know how to shoot properly."

"It only takes one shot," said John.

"Well," said Dale. "I just take life as it comes. If they come at me, they'll be dealing not just with me and my guns, but with Kiki, too. Don't let her fool you. She can be fierce when she wants to."

John gazed down at Kiki. She was a sizable animal, and muscular. "I don't doubt that one bit. But..." John went on to tell Dale a little about the farmhouse where they'd been staying. Cynthia interjected occasionally to add comments and details. Together, they told Dale about what had happened in the suburbs, and how the militia was expanding its reach. And about how the farmhouse had already been overrun with people fleeing the cities, dangerous people who'd do anything to get ahead, to ensure another minute of their own survival.

"Don't worry, kid," said Dale. (This was the first time John had been called a kid in decades.) "I know what I'm doing. I'm willing to take the risks. This is the life I want.

And it's the life I'm going to live. Plus, I've got communication with the outside world."

"You do?" said Cynthia. "How's that possible?"

"I've got a radio."

"A radio?"

"Yup, a shortwave radio. Reminds me of my trucker days. Although those were CBs, of course. Same idea, though, messages traveling through the air and all that."

"But wait, you don't even have electricity here."

"I've got some. Just for special occasions. I've got a car battery rigged up..."

"But you'd need a..."

"A Faraday cage, yup. I keep it inside it, just in case there's another EMP. Although I don't see what the point of another one would be. Everything's already knocked out, from what I hear."

"A Faraday cage, that's incredible," said John. "So you were planning for an EMP?"

"Not planning for it. Just expecting the worst. It's part of my personality, in a way, to meet what's coming cheerfully and with the best-laid plans as I possibly can."

John didn't see how that mindset meshed with failing to acknowledge the threat that the militia posed to his own safety, but he was in Dale's own house, and he wasn't going to argue the point with him anymore.

"You know they're looking for a radio, don't you?" said John. He couldn't keep this point to himself. "The militia, I mean." Somehow he knew that Dale already knew, and had already known everything that John had so patiently explained to him.

"Oh, sure," said Dale. "But they don't know I've got it. And even if they did, they'd have a hell of a time finding me. I don't make any transmissions myself."

"You just listen?"

"You mean there are people out there?" said Cynthia, her jaw dropping as she finally understood the implications. "People... elsewhere?"

"Yup," said Dale. "Not many of them. I listen to two broadcasts. Pretty short ones. There's a community in New York state that I pick up, and another in Ohio. There's another one somewhere around, but I haven't found them yet. Apparently they're very secretive about their location."

"Can we see it?" said John. "Can we listen?"

John was eager to hear something of the outside world. It would be just a little slice of sound, but it would make him feel... connected again. The way he'd been before the EMP, with the internet at his fingertips, with his smartphone always in his pocket.

"Well, there's nothing now," said Dale. "No broadcasts scheduled, as far as I'm aware. Nothing but static. We can listen first thing in the morning, though. The place in New York will be sending something out."

John nodded. That was good enough for him. It was something to look forward to. How the world had changed—he now considered a few minutes of a person's voice on the radio a little jewel, a little sliver of hope.

"Now," said Dale. "I imagine after all this talking, you two are starting to work up an appetite again."

Cynthia nodded eagerly.

"I don't think it's fair that we eat your food," said John. "I mean, I really appreciate it, but you're already doing so much by letting us stay here. We've got some food left, some energy bars and things like that."

"Nonsense, I've got plenty. And you're having some. No arguing." Dale laughed like this was the funniest thing in the whole world. "I've got a whole root cellar packed to the gills. And it's hidden real good, too, so don't think anyone's going to find it. When I'm feeling chipper, I'll just be out hunting some deer, supposing they decide to pass by."

"I wish I could have your attitude about things," muttered John, looking down at his feet.

"Hey, you've had it harder than I have. I'm a lucky man and I know that, and that's why I'm willing to share with good people like yourselves."

John nodded without saying anything.

Dale got out a huge cast iron pan and put it directly onto the wood stove.

"These are venison sausages," he said, holding them out for John and Cynthia to see, before adding them to the pan, along with a healthy amount of butter. "These will have you feeling better than you've felt in a long time, trust me. Loaded with nutrients."

John and Cynthia fell silent as Dale banged around the kitchen, chuckling to himself over this or that. Who knew, really, what inspired his laughter.

Before he knew it, John had fallen fast asleep in his chair. It's been so long since he'd sat in one that he'd almost forgotten how comfortable they were, and how easy it was to fall asleep in one.

The next thing he knew, Dale was thrusting a plate of steaming venison sausages into his hands and clapping him on the shoulder to wake him up.

John looked up and saw Cynthia beaming at him, her mouth already full of sausage.

The three of them chatted through dinner, enjoying the sausages immensely.

Now, with the rabbit and the sausages together in a

single day, John had eaten better than he had in a long, long time. It was almost more protein than his body knew what to do with. He hoped it would store it away for a future time, when the meals would be lean and miserable again, when they'd be tightening their belts and soldiering on to some new and dangerous land.

The conversation turned this way and that, and somehow Dale always steered it away from the new world that they lived in. Nothing bleak was talked about. Nothing horrible. Nothing tragic. Instead, they talked about things they'd read, things they'd heard, things they'd seen on television. Dale was particularly fond of retelling funny conversations he'd overheard in highway rest stops all over the country. As a truck driver, he'd been over practically every inch of the country, always with his ear cocked and his eyes open for comedic situations. Or at least what he considered comedic situations. He seemed to see the humor in everything, even when others would recoil in horror or disgust.

It was pleasant and convivial, sitting there in good company, enjoying a chat that had nothing to do with surviving, nothing to do with what was needed to be done.

John knew, though, that it was only the briefest of respites. Soon, they'd be back on the trail, heading to who knew where. Soon all the conversations would turn again to guns and watches and food rationing.

30

MANDY

Mandy couldn't believe that they were out of there. She couldn't believe they were alive.

They'd barreled down the back roads in the Bronco. Mandy had been terrified, behind the wheel, her foot not letting up on the gas pedal for a second. She hadn't had any idea where she was taking them. The only thing she'd known was that she'd needed to get as far away from the compound as they could.

Mandy had driven down dusty back roads on tree-lined streets, through the middle of the night. She'd driven until they'd run out of gas.

The backseat had been full of frantic activity. They'd been trying to treat Georgia's bullet wound.

Georgia had woken up. She'd been in incredible pain, trying to grit her teeth. But she'd had to scream. It'd been inevitable. The pain would have been too much for anyone.

Mandy had kept her eyes on the road as much as possible, but when she'd glanced in the rearview mirror, she'd seen nothing but bloodied hands and a sweating Georgia, her face contorted in pure pain.

Somehow, Max had gotten the bullet out. James had been fishing through the gear constantly, finding things for Max, acting as the dutiful and silent doctor's assistant.

And there in the backseat, Max had performed the procedure, in silent concentration, with only a few words here and there to James.

Sadie hadn't been able to turn around and watch. She'd sat there with her eyes closed, her knees pulled up to her chest, shaking in fear of losing her mother.

Eventually, the Bronco had simply run out of gas. There was nothing there except the trees. No nearby towns. Nothing. They had no idea where they were.

They stayed in the Bronco through the night. A sleepless night. Mandy kept her hand on her gun the entire time. Unfortunately, most of their ammo had been stolen. They'd had it all with them in their packs—none of it had been left in the Bronco, for fear of it getting stolen. So all Mandy had was what she'd taken from the guard Georgia had shot.

If it hadn't been for Georgia, they'd all have been dead. They'd never have made it. Not even Max. Because he would have busted into the compound no matter what, and Max would have died there if Mandy and the others hadn't been alive when he'd come in.

As the sun rose, Max finally stepped down out of the Bronco and joined Mandy at the rear bumper, which she leaned on.

"How's she doing?" whispered Mandy.

"Not good," said Max. A grim look was on his battered face.

"Is she going to make it?"

"I hope so."

"That doesn't mean much."

"No. It doesn't. I got the bullet out, but she's sick. She's running a high fever."

"What can we do?"

"Nothing. Nothing I know of."

"What do we do?"

"Wait."

Mandy nodded in the early morning light. There wasn't anything else to say about Georgia. Either she'd live or she wouldn't. It was out of their hands. They could bring her water and stay by her. They could give her antibiotics. They could hope for the best. But after that, it was out of their hands.

Mandy hoped she'd live, but she didn't dare say it out loud.

Max and Mandy stood there, staring off into the sky together, side by side, not speaking. They'd been through so much that it seemed to have taken all the words right out of them. It'd taken more than words, but it was hard to say exactly what.

Several minutes passed.

"You think we'll make it?" said Mandy, finally.

Max didn't answer. Instead, he turned his face towards her and looked her right in the eyes.

His eyes were bloodshot as hers probably were, from too many nights without sleep, from too many days without food. Viciously dark circles hung under each eye. The injuries on his face, rather than looking better, were now looking worse than ever. He'd been drenched in sweat and blood, a thin film of grime building up over the bruises, never getting washed off.

But in his eyes... there was something. Something

powerful. It wasn't hope. No, it wasn't anything like that. But in his eyes Mandy saw Max's drive. She saw his will to live. To continue.

And that was all Mandy needed. That was her answer.

Max hadn't lost it.

And, as Mandy now realized, neither had she.

They'd make it, whether or not Georgia made it.

"We're going to have to make camp here," said Max. "Did you figure out where we are yet?"

Mandy shook her head. "We might have crossed into West Virginia. I don't know. But we went west, as far as I can tell. Unless I took some crazy switchbacks and didn't realize it."

"You did good with the driving."

Mandy nodded. She wasn't so sure she'd done a good job, but at least she'd done it.

"We need to get the Bronco off of the road, out of view, in case anyone comes by."

"We're going to camp with the Bronco? Why don't we just leave it and hike to a new spot, away from it?"

"We need to keep Georgia in there, I think," said Max. "I don't think we should move her. It's getting cold at night, and it's going to be better shelter than anything we'll be able to build."

"How are we going to get it into the woods, though?"

Max surveyed the surrounding area briefly. "Push it, I guess. We can push it over some of the saplings. I'll try to find a path without any big trees in the way, wide enough for the Bronco."

"If you say so."

Mandy knew now that Max's instincts were... well, they weren't always right. But they were worth following.

No one, after all, could be right all the time. Not since the EMP. There were too many unknowns.

"Check on Georgia, will you?" said Max, starting to walk off in search of a path for the Bronco.

"Max," said Mandy.

She reached out and grabbed his torn coat sleeve.

"What is it?"

Mandy held on to Max. She didn't want to let him go, even though he'd be back momentarily.

But she didn't know what to say. She wanted to tell him how she felt about him, but she couldn't get the words out.

"Nothing," she said.

"You OK?"

"I guess."

Max nodded, turned, and headed off. In their current situation, "I guess" was about as good as it was going to get.

Mandy stood there for a moment watching Max's back. He walked with a slight limp now. Obviously the leg was still painful. But it was amazing he was walking at all.

The air had a bite to it, and Mandy put her hands into the pockets of her coat, only to find that they'd torn, just like the rest of the coat. A strange memory came flooding back to her. It was just a fragment, really. A fragment of a poem she'd had to memorize back in high school for French class. She couldn't remember the French, but the English translation she remembered went something like, "I put my hands in my torn pockets. My overcoat, too, was becoming ideal."

The author was Rimbaud, some French poet who she couldn't remember anything about.

For Mandy, the poet had been trying to say that he'd

like the adventure of life, the turmoil and the insults, the hardships and the lean times.

It was pure romanticism.

Mandy had liked the poem. She'd even had a brief phase as a teenager of wearing torn jeans, mostly because of that poem, and partly because it looked cool and was stylish at the time.

But now that times really were lean, the romanticism meant nothing to her.

No, she didn't long for the times before the EMP. But that wasn't because she wouldn't have preferred them. It was simply because that world was gone. Probably never to return. There wasn't any point in thinking about it.

Mandy, along with the others, had been transformed. Transformed into a person she never would have recognized before the EMP.

Mandy didn't have time to stay lost in daydreams. There were things to be done.

"How's she doing?" said Mandy, opening the back door to the Bronco.

Georgia lay there, on her stomach. Max had stopped the bleeding by suturing the wound. He'd done it somewhat crudely. After all, he wasn't a doctor. But it had worked.

"Better," said James. He sounded tired and worried. But he was keeping it together. "But she's still got a fever."

Mandy nodded.

Georgia wasn't unconscious, but she wasn't speaking either.

"The antibiotics will work," said Mandy. "You need some rest, James. Let me take care of your mom for now."

James shook his head.

She could see in his eyes that there wasn't any way to convince him otherwise.

Through the rear windshield, which had at least one bullet hole, Mandy saw Max reappearing.

"How's she doing?"

"The same, I think."

"Let's hope those antibiotics work."

They spoke in hushed tones, so that James couldn't hear them from inside the Bronco.

"I found a place we can push it."

"It's going to be hard, pushing it over that terrain. You think we can do it?"

"We have to."

"We better do it now, before we lose any more energy."

"We need to clear some saplings first. Some are too big for the car."

"But we don't have an ax."

"I think we can take them with the knives. Come on, I need your help. You have your Mora?"

"Always do." Mandy patted the plastic-sheathed knife on her belt. It had been a literal life-saver at least once. And probably would be again.

Mandy ducked her head back into the Bronco to tell James and Sadie what was going on. "Keep on the lookout," said Mandy. "I know you want to keep your eyes on your mom, but you also need to be ready for someone coming. Let's hope that doesn't happen, though."

James gave a stiff nod. Sadie was still mostly unresponsive in the front seat, overcome with stress and worry.

Mandy set off to follow Max, who was already walking back to where he'd found the place to forge a trail. It was about 200 feet from the Bronco.

When Mandy caught up with him, he was already at

work, using his pocket knife to splice into the saplings. Mandy watched how he moved the knife up and down, rocking it, and then bent the sapling until it snapped.

Mandy tried to do the same with her own knife, but it was hard at first.

"There's a trick to it," said Max, observing her. "Only make one cut. You just want to rock it. Don't try to saw it."

"OK, I think I got it."

Max nodded, as she snapped her first sapling.

"Max," said Mandy. "We haven't talked about Chad."

Max was silent for a moment. "What's there to talk about?"

"I don't know... He was your friend, from way back."

Max nodded.

"And, I don't know. If you wanted to talk to me about it, that'd be fine. I'm here for you."

"Thanks, but words aren't going to bring him back. He's dead, and that's it."

Mandy didn't say anything. Max was already back at work.

Max had found the perfect spot. Along most of the road, there were thick trees that they couldn't cut down, but right here, where they stood, there was just enough space for the Bronco to fit. Why there were saplings, Mandy didn't know. She didn't have time to think about it, since it was hard work. There wasn't much in the way of bushes, but there were plenty of rocks, which, along with the uneven ground, made the work harder than it would have been. And it would make pushing the Bronco even harder.

It took them a good twenty minutes to get the path clear enough that the Bronco would be able to travel over the ground.

"Come on," said Max. "We might as well get this over with. It's going to be a hell of a job pushing it down here."

"You think it's far enough?"

Max nodded. "Yeah, we'll be mostly out of view. We can set up camp there."

"And then what? We're not going to be able to travel without gas." It was obvious, but Mandy felt she needed to say it anyway. She wanted to get Max's take on what would happen.

"We can't all hike out. Not with Georgia like this."

That was obvious, too.

"So we're going to just stay here?"

"For a while. Until Georgia's better. If she makes it, that is. Come on, time to push the Bronco."

Mandy's muscles were already weak and tired. She didn't feel like she had the strength to walk back to the Bronco, let alone push it, with Georgia and the gear inside it, across uneven terrain.

31

JOHN

John woke up early in the morning. Sunlight came through the small windows of Dale's cabin.

He was a little stiff, but not too bad. He felt stronger than he had yesterday. A lot stronger. He was regaining his strength.

It had been a long time since John had felt so rested. He'd spent the night in the chair, something that months ago he would have thought sounded far too uncomfortable. But it was better than the uneven ground out in the woods. It was better than sleeping on rocks, or not sleeping at all.

He'd only woken up twice that night. Normally, when he and Cynthia had slept outside, he'd never go a full night without waking up a dozen times, his heart pounding, fearing that some attack was looming immediately, close and deadly.

But it had only been Kiki, barking loudly and deeply, that had woken him up. Each time, she'd settled down soon enough, lying back down on the wooden floorboards of the cabin.

They hadn't kept a watch, which had felt strange and dangerous to John and Cynthia. But Dale had assured them there was nothing to worry about, that Kiki was a better watchman than any human under the sun. They'd been so tired, and John so weak, that they didn't have it in them to protest.

John looked around. Dale and Kiki were gone, probably on a walk around the property.

Cynthia snored lightly nearby, curled up in her wooden chair. She looked cute like that, almost beautiful. Her hair had come undone from her braid, and it hung messily around her, the sunlight hitting it just right.

John got up silently, so as not to wake Cynthia. He had to urinate, and, looking around, there didn't seem to be any kind of bathroom facilities. Not that he would have expected any in a cabin like this. But he hadn't seen an outhouse either.

That was fine with John. He'd do what he'd done since the EMP, and go in the great outdoors.

John patted his gun on his hip before opening the door as quietly as he could. He took one last look at Cynthia to make sure he hadn't woken her up before stepping outside.

The air had a chilly bite to it. The sun was still low in the sky and hadn't yet started to warm everything up.

John cast his eyes around. Everything looked peaceful and calm. The trees swayed slightly in an early morning breeze.

John found his way along a narrow path that wound its way through the trees. He stepped off the path, so as not to leave urine on the path itself, unzipped his pants, and breathed a sigh of relief.

He'd had a lot of tea last night, and the stream continued and continued, seemingly relentlessly.

There was a sound off to his right. A twig cracking, or something similar.

John turned his head sharply, but he saw nothing.

Must have just been an animal. A squirrel or rabbit.

Nothing but quiet, now.

John must have imagined it. He was still jumpy, though, and on guard, considering that he knew for a fact there were two criminals out there with firearms. Sure, they may have headed off in some other direction. That was what he was hoping for.

John finally finished, and his early morning cold fingers found the zipper with some difficulty.

As he was zipping up, a tremendous bang rang out in the forest.

It was a gunshot. It came from over where he'd heard the twig snapping.

The bullet smashed into a tree a mere foot from his head. Wood splinters exploded outward from the tree. John felt some of them hit his shirt.

John threw himself to the ground. Quickly and instinctively. His hand reached for his gun.

It felt good in his hand. Cold and firm.

On his belly, he thrust the gun in front of him, holding it with both hands. His eyes darted back and forth, trying to find the attacker.

A flash of movement up ahead. An orange jumpsuit. Unmistakable. So it was the criminals. Or one of them, at least.

John knew that if there was one there, there'd be another one nearby. Shit. He might get attacked from behind. He'd never know it until it was too late.

It was good John and Cynthia had been practicing so much with the firearms. He certainly was still no expert, but he was a lot better. Everything about the gun felt natural to John now, and he felt confident he could hit the guy, provided he could just get a clear shot.

The orange jumpsuit was hidden behind a tree. But the guy would have to move. He couldn't stay there forever.

John kept his eyes on the tree the jumpsuit had disappeared behind. If he took his eyes off to check for another attacker, he'd risk losing his chance of getting a shot off.

So he kept his ears peeled, listening as close as he could for sounds coming from any direction.

A flash of the orange jumpsuit up ahead.

John was ready.

He squeezed the trigger.

The other guy didn't stand a chance. He didn't even have time to get off a shot.

He collapsed to the ground. John's round hit him square in the chest.

Somewhere, off in the forest, a dog barked. It had to be Kiki.

John spun around.

The other convict was there, his hand gripping a pistol, rising up to point the gun at John. It seemed to happen in slow motion.

Before John could throw himself onto the ground, a crack rang out. Another shot had been fired.

The convict fell, his heavy body hitting the ground with a soft thud. Blood poured from his head.

Dale stood off in the distance, partially obscured by a tree. He held a rifle, the scope pushed to his eye. He lowered the rifle.

"Not a bad shot, eh?" called out Dale. "There were only two of them, right?"

"Just two, yeah."

Dale was striding over.

Kiki got to John before Dale did. She came up and started licking his hand.

"Good girl, good girl," said John.

"You feeling all right?" said Dale, clapping John on the back.

"Better than yesterday, that's for sure."

"How's that arm doing?"

"Feels fine. I'll get Cynthia to take another look at it today. Thanks, by the way. You've saved my life. Maybe twice now."

"Don't think anything of it," said Dale. "It wasn't a hard shot. Come on, let's go see if we can tune into that broadcast."

John felt excitement bubbling up in his chest. The convicts had made him briefly forget about it, and the excitement he'd felt last night about the possibility of hearing someone's voice piping through a radio.

"What about the bodies?"

"I'll take care of them later," said Dale. "Come on."

John turned to follow Dale towards the cabin.

"Everyone all right?" called out an unseen Cynthia.

"We're fine," yelled Dale happily. "Just took care of some scumbags. We each got one. Not bad for an early morning session."

Cynthia stepped out from behind a tree where she'd been hiding. She was holding her handgun, ready to shoot.

"I couldn't tell what was happening," she said. "I heard gunshots, and didn't know who'd been shot."

"You did the right thing by staying hidden. I could have been dead. It wouldn't have done any good to come running," said John.

"You don't need to tell me that. Why do you think I stayed hidden?"

"She's a fiery one," chuckled Dale. "Come on, before we miss the broadcast."

They followed Dale inside, and Kiki followed them.

"Now first Kiki needs a little treat," said Dale, taking one of the sausages from last night and tossing it to Kiki, who caught it in mid-air. "And now, for the moment we've all been waiting for."

John and Cynthia sat back in their wooden chairs, the same ones they'd slept in, and watched anxiously as Dale opened a big wooden trunk that was tucked away in one of the corners of the small cabin.

"Now it may not look fancy, this Faraday cage of mine, but trust me, it does the trick."

It was homemade, and looked like pieces of chicken-wire had been smushed together.

Dale struggled briefly with the mesh, but he got the radio out.

"Standard shortwave radio," he said. "Nothing fancy. But it works, which is more than you can say about most of these radios. Now, let's see, we've got one minute. Good timing."

"Why does your watch still work?" said Cynthia, apparently noticing for the first time that Dale wore a working watch.

"No batteries," said Dale, grinning. "It's a mechanical watch. Not a drop of electricity in the whole thing. Old Russian military watch. Won it during a card game twenty years ago, and it's been going strong ever since. Tough as nails, too."

Dale was fiddling with the radio and glancing at his watch, watching the red second hand ticking across the blue dial, on which, inexplicably, was a picture of a scuba diver.

"OK, here goes nothing. Quiet, everyone."

John and Cynthia didn't need to be told. They didn't know what they'd hear. But really, anything would be something. Anything would be a spark of hope. Hope that there were others out there, working on rebuilding something, even if it was something as simple as a rudimentary communication network.

The radio hissed and crackled.

Someone's voice came through. It was a woman's voice. She sounded young, around college age, but it was hard to tell with all the static.

"Zoe coming at you today. Hope you're all ready for the exciting updates of this beautiful Tuesday here in upstate New York... undisclosed location, of course..."

A brief hiss of static obscured the announcer's words momentarily.

"Hope you're all hunkering down and surviving as best you can. I know we've all been working on our canning here. Lots of berries to preserve for the coming winter. Make sure you've all got your gear ready and don't forget to air it out. Just because we don't have traditional showers, and just because no one's using deodorant, doesn't mean we all have to stink any more than we have to. And yes, I'm referring to you, Ted. Now... OK, they're telling me I have to get onto the—" another hiss of static "—and that wraps it up for that little sad announcement, but as I've said over and over, there's not much good news these days. But we'll take what we can get when we can get it."

Dale was chuckling, muttering, "That girl's really something."

John and Cynthia glanced at each other. They didn't know what to make of the announcement so far. It was silly and kind of goofy, in an offbeat kind of tone that belied the experiences they'd had so far.

John and Cynthia had struggled. They'd almost been killed who knew how many times. And they'd had to shoot to kill. They were dirty and mud streaked and blood stained. But this young woman on the radio was cracking jokes and talking about preserving berries.

"And now we're going to get to the list... so far we haven't learned of connecting anyone together. But if you're out there listening, maybe you'll hear of a family member or friend who's still alive. An unnamed community in an unknown location in Pennsylvania recently had the following visitors, who apparently refused to give their full names. Now that's not much good for most, but maybe you'll know the whole group, and be able to identify them by their first names. I really have no idea."

More static hissed through the radio.

"So to repeat that list, we have: Max, Mandy, Georgia, Chad, Sadie, and James. OK, folks, that about wraps it up. We'll be on the air again Thursday. Same time, same channel. Keep a cool head, and keep those guns within arm's reach. Over and out."

"Hell of a program, right?" said Dale.

Max and Chad...

John couldn't believe it.

Max and Chad. In Pennsylvania. There was no way it wasn't his brother and his childhood friend.

"Cat got your tongue or something?" said Dale.

Cynthia was staring at him. "You think that's your brother? Wasn't he named Max?"

"It's definitely my brother," said John. "I know Chad, too. No idea what he's doing with Max... but... he's alive."

"That's your brother?" said Dale.

John nodded.

He felt, for the first time in a while, that there was some hope for himself and Cynthia. He didn't know why the news of Max gave him hope, but it did.

"Too bad we don't know where he is," said Cynthia.

"You don't know where the other community is, do you?" said John, looking at Dale.

Dale shook his head. "Nope, nobody does. But I could hazard a guess."

"A guess?"

"Well, there aren't too many spots where I'd make one if I was the type to start up a community. If I wasn't such a solitary guy, you know. And there were rumors for a few years of one... people were setting something up, some group... I forget off the top of my head."

"Do you have it written down or anything? Or on a map?"

Dale laughed. "Nope. I've never been one to keep things on paper. Everything's up here." He tapped his head with his knuckles. "Except for when I forget it."

John didn't know what to say. For a brief moment, it had seemed like he might be able to find Max. Now that hope was dashed.

"How'd you hear those rumors?" said Cynthia.

"Oh, a friend in town," said Dale. "Haven't seen him since the EMP. But he'd probably still know, if he's still alive."

Cynthia and John looked at each other.

"Are you thinking what I'm thinking?"

"I think so."

"You really want to find your brother?" said Dale.

John nodded.

"From what John tells me," said Cynthia, "he'd be a big help to our survival."

"Yeah," muttered John. "But that was back when we thought he was at the farmhouse... Now, I don't know..."

"I think we should try to find him," said Cynthia.

"You think so?"

"Hell," said Dale. "If I had a brother, and knew he was alive, I'd try to find him, even if he knew shit about surviving."

John made the decision in an instant. "All right," he said. "We'll do it. At the very least, if we can find this community, maybe it's a place we could fit into. Even if Max isn't still there. You in, Cynthia?"

Cynthia nodded.

"OK," said John. "Looks like we've got ourselves a plan. For now, at least."

"Stay for another day," said Dale. "I'll get you two well fed, and get some extra food ready for you to take."

"You've done enough already," said Cynthia.

Dale smiled. "I've got plenty," he said. "And I want to help. So the wise thing to do would be to take what I give you."

"Can't argue with that, I guess."

"You know what," said Dale. "Maybe I'll come with you two. Just to the town, that is. I'll introduce you to Harry. He can be a cranky old geezer, but he sure as hell always knows what's going on. Has his ear to the ground, so to speak."

Cynthia looked at John, probably expecting him to decline.

"That'd be great," said John, knowing that Dale would be a good man to have along.

32

MAX

Max and Mandy stood on the outskirts of the little campsite. It'd been a week since they'd gotten here, and in a strange way it had started to feel like home.

Max and Mandy spoke in quiet, hushed voices. They stood close together, both facing the campsite. They were dirty, tired, and hungry.

It was early morning, and Sadie and James's snores could be heard from the Bronco.

"How's Georgia doing today?" said Max.

"About the same. She's going to live. And she'll be able to walk and move. But it's going to take a while. She needs time."

"I guess that's good."

"She's not getting worse. That's a good sign. The antibiotics helped. No infection, from what I can tell. The fever's been gone for three days. You did a good job getting the bullet out."

"I hope so. All that reading I did before the EMP paid off."

"It's going to be a lot longer before she's able to walk."

"I know. Maybe weeks."

"Maybe more," said Mandy.

"She's not going to get any better without food."

"We're running low..."

"You don't need to tell me that."

There was practically no food left. Fortunately, a small creek ran nearby, and they had enough water.

Max had set up some traps, like the ones Jeff had shown him. He'd caught a couple squirrels, but nothing bigger than that. And squirrels didn't provide a lot of meat.

"Still no sign of any deer?"

Max shook his head. "Not unless you've seen any."

"Nope, nothing."

"We only have the handguns to hunt with anyway, and ammo is low."

Mandy nodded. "What are we going to do?"

"I've been thinking," said Max, "that the best thing is if I go find some gas."

"You? Alone?"

Max nodded. "They need you here. You're the only functional adult now. You'll be able to catch more squirrels in the traps. Without me, it'll be one less mouth to feed. You'll be fine until I get back."

"I don't like the idea of you going alone, though. And why now? It doesn't seem like we should leave yet. There haven't been any cars that have come by. It doesn't seem like they're looking for us."

"It might take me a while," said Max. "Who knows where I'll be able to find gas, and how long it'll take me to get there and back. Once Georgia's ready, we need to be ready to go. We'll need the gas. We can't stay here any longer than we have to. We're too close to the compound, and food is scarce."

"You mean it might take you days?"

"Hopefully. Maybe weeks. There could be a car with gas a mile away, or a hundred. We don't even know where we are. There was nothing but woods when we were driving out here. I didn't see any towns."

"I don't think you should go alone."

Mandy wore a pained expression on her face.

"I have to."

Max looked into Mandy's eyes and saw that she knew it was the truth. There wasn't any other way.

"When are you going to go?"

"The sooner the better. My bag's already packed."

"You mean today?"

"I mean now."

"Now?"

"Right now, yeah."

"You're tired. You should rest first."

Max just shook his head. "It'll be better if you say goodbye to the others for me."

"Max..."

"I'm doing this for all of us," said Max.

Mandy took his hand in hers, and held it for a moment.

But she let it slip away as Max turned and walked to his pack, which he'd prepared during the night. He'd packed only a small amount of food, leaving most of what was left for the others.

Max shouldered his pack.

Mandy didn't wave, and neither did Max. They looked at each other for a moment, and then Max turned and set off towards the road. The camp wasn't visible from the road, so Max would leave himself a marker, something that only he would recognize.

It might be a long road ahead, but Max was ready.

They'd survived. That was the important thing. And they'd continue to survive. Max would do everything he could. And he knew the others would too. They'd made mistakes. Max had made many. But that's the way life was now—it wasn't a straight easy path from one point to the next.

WANT to know when book 4 is coming out? Receive *Surviving the Crash*, a free short story about the EMP, when you sign up for my mailing list: http://eepurl.com/c8UeN5

ABOUT RYAN WESTFIELD

Ryan Westfield is an author of post-apocalyptic survival thrillers. He's always had an interest in "being prepared," and spends time wondering what that really means. When he's not writing and reading, he enjoys being outdoors.

Contact Ryan at ryan@ryanwestfield.com